P9-CEL-716

The Fullmetal Alchemist Archive

The Complete Guide

cocoro books

Published by DH Publishing, Inc.
1-3-16-4F Komagata, Taito-Ku
Tokyo 111-0043, Japan
http://www.dhp-online.com
cocoro books is an imprint of DH Publishing, Inc.

First Published 2007

Text and illustrations ©2007 by DH Publishing, Inc.

Printed in CHINA

Printed by Miyuki Inter-Media Hong Kong, Inc.
Compiled by Kazuhisa Fujie, Matthew Lane and Walt Wyman
Publisher: Hiroshi Yokoi
Editor: Kazuhisa Fujie
ISBN 978-1-932897-20-3
By courtesy of Akio Kurono (cac co,ltd.)

The Fullmetal Alchemist Archive

How to Use

In this book, the ninth in the popular Mysteries and Secrets Revealed! series, you'll find everything you need to know about the Fullmetal Alchemist and much more! And it's so easy to use…just follow the Fullmetal Alchemist code below and within a few hours you will be an Alchemist expert!

Questions and Answers

Want to find out why who did what when and where? Then this is the book for you. Includes 73 questions and detailed answers on every Fullmetal Alchemist topic, from fighting techniques to character backgrounds and history.

Glossary

When you speak the lingo everything is so much easier. At the back of this book you will find all of the characters that make an appearance in the series along with a comprehensive list of techniques.

Keyword Index

Want to go straight to Konohagakure State Alchemist? Then start at the alphabetical Keyword Index at the back of the book. There you'll find page links to every destination, character and technique in the Fullmetal Alchemist world.

Overview

Fullmetal Alchemist (Japanese title: Haganeno Renkinjutsushi, or Hagaren for short) is a manga by Hiromu Arakawa serialized in Monthly Shonen Gangan. It also refers to the television anime series of the same name. It is serialized in Monthly Shonen Gangan (Square Enix). The first 13 volumes have sold 20 million copies. It won 2004 49th Shogakukan Mangasho (Shogakukan Manga Award). This was the second time a Square Enix comic had received the award (first was Igarashi Mikio's Ninpen Manmaru). As of this writing (2006), the manga is on its 14th volume.

In keeping with Square Enix's multi-format marketing, an FMA animated series, video games and movie were created. There are many differences in the story and characters between the manga and anime.

Story overview

The Elric brothers, Edward and Alphonse, attempt to resurrect their dead mother using the forbidden alchemic practice of human transmutation. The transmutation fails and Edward (11) loses his left arm while his younger brother Alphonse (10) loses his entire body. Edward sacrifices his right arm to bring back Alphonse's soul and bind it to a suit of armor. Edward becomes a State Alchemist with the title "Fullmetal Alchemist" at age 12, and embarks on a journey to find the Philosopher's Stone in order to return Alphonse to his body. However, numerous hardships await the Elric brothers on their journeys. Out-gunned by their numerous enemies, the brother's bond deepens as they search for their prize.

CONTENTS

Homunculus' Secrets

PART 01

FMA's Secrets

The Fullmetal Alchemist manga began running as a serial in Square Enix's comic digest Monthly Shonen Gangan (hereafter, Gangan) in 2001. The series' creator, Hiromu Arakawa, was a newcomer at the time. The series was a hit, and actually became so popular that it pushed up sales of Gangan. The compilation volumes also sold well, and the series is still running as of this writing (2007). In 2004, FMA won the prestigious Shogakukan Mangasho (Shogakukan Manga Award).

Regarding the anime, Mainichi Broadcasting System arranged to broadcast an animated version of the series, choosing Bones Co. Ltd., a comparatively new anime studio founded in 1998, to handle the animation. The animated series spanned 51 episodes, running from October 4, 2003 until October 2, 2004. At its peak, it had a viewer rating of 16%, which is considered high for an anime series in Japan. In 2004, the animated series won the Award for Outstanding Animated Work in the Television Category at the Tokyo International Anime Fair. The script and voice acting also received accolades. In 2005, the series ranked 20th in an anime popularity survey taken by TV Asahi. In an online survey, the series ranked No. 1, beating Mobile Suit Gundam by over 1000 votes.

In the beginning, the manga and anime ran parallel to each other, and the script for the animated series was created jointly by the Bones staff and Arakawa. However, the anime was scheduled to be broadcast for just one year, so its story had to be wrapped up before that of the manga. As a result, the anime story diverges from that of the manga midway through the series. Apparently, Arakawa was not very satisfied with the original story and ending for the anime series. As for other differences, many of the characters are completely different in the manga and anime, although they share the same names. The Philosopher's Stones are also portrayed differently. As described above, the manga and anime were created under different circumstances and follow different stories. This has led many Japanese fans to consider them to be two different works.

In July 2005, Fullmetal Alchemist the Movie: Conqueror of Shamballa opened in theaters in Japan. Billed as a sequel to the television series, it went on to sell around a million tickets. Clearly then, the anime has also enjoyed high popularity as an independent work. This book predominantly relies on the manga as its source material. However, whenever possible, additional explanations are given in cases where the manga and anime diverge.

See Glossary

Square Enix
Shonen Gangan
Hiromu Arakawa
Bones

02 What sort of company is Bones (the studio that created the FMA anime)?

Bones was founded in October 1998 by Masahiko Minami, Koji Ousaka and Toshihiro Kawamoto. These three had previously worked at Sunrise (the company responsible for producing the Mobile Suit Gundam series). Minami was formerly a producer, while Ousaka and Kawamoto were animators. The name derives from a Japanese idiom "hone no aru," literally "to have bones," meaning "having backbone/spirit" or "solid" etc. In Japan the company is known for having very high standards when it comes to its staff. The company's artistic capabilities and ability to create elaborate stories has garnered it praise both in Japan and abroad. In addition to FMA, some of the company's representative works are Karakuri Kiden Hiwou Senki, Kidou Tenshi Angelic Layer, Eureka 7, etc. For FMA, Bones expanded on the themes of life and death addressed by the manga, revealing in depth the Law of Equivalent Exchange.

The result was an original storyline that surprised many of the manga's fans and stirred up controversy. Supporters of the anime pointed to the well-developed storyline. Critics felt the anime's story was too dark where it should have been more light-hearted.

ee Glossary

Bones
Masahiro Minami
Koji Ousaka
Toshihiro Kawamoto

See questions
01

S quare Enix is indeed a game publisher that has produced many hit series including Final Fantasy and Dragon Quest. As the name indicates, it was once two companies--Square and Enix--which merged in 2003. Originally published by Enix, Monthly Shonen Gangan began running in 1991, before the merger. It was distinguished by its fantasy-oriented manga, which is as one might expect from a company that specialized in role-playing games.

In June 2001, Enix spun off a part of Gangan's editorial staff to form Mag Garden Corporation. The spin-off company brought with it the top artists from Gangan in order to work on a new digest--Monthly Comic Blade. With its most popular artists gone, Gangan was in serious danger of being discontinued, but with the success of FMA, sales have recovered. Due to the merger with Square, Gangan now also carries a manga based on the Final Fantasy game series.

Gangan is famous for being one of the thicker manga digests. A common joke among fans is that you could kill someone with it, use it as an improvised bludgeon, etc.

See Glossary

Shonen Gangan
Square Enix
Final Fantasy
Dragon Quest

See questions
01 **04** **09**

04 How did Hiromu Arakawa come to create FMA?

A rakawa, FMA's creator, comes from Hokkaido. She moved to Tokyo to become a manga artist, and worked as an assistant to Hiroyuki Etou on the series Mahojin Guruguru, which ran in Gangan from 1992 to August 2003. She produced some comic strips under the alias Edmond Arakawa, but her debut as Hiromu Arakawa came with a one-shot manga called Stray Dog, which ran in Gangan in 1999. After this, she continued releasing short works, including Totsugeki Tonari no Enikkusu, and Shanghai Makikai in Gangan.

FMA too was originally slated as a one-shot manga for Gangan, but after seeing a storyboard, the editor asked her to turn it into a serial. Having only ever worked with short episodes, Arakawa felt out of place. In Japan it is quite rare for a new artist to have her own serial. However, wanting to make the most of this opportunity, she worked hard for two weeks to reshape the plot. The serial was a hit from the beginning. Newbie Arakawa had not only produced a work that put her on the map, she had created a work assured of classic status in the annals of Japanese manga.

In rethinking the plot, Arakawa apparently came up with the conclusion first. With the end already in mind, she approaches each installment with the intention of showing growth in the characters as they move on in their journey. Regarding serial manga, she was quoted as saying: "Those manga that keep you holding your breath the whole time tire me out. Manga are entertainment. They should be fun to read. Remembering the manga I read as a kid, there were some I enjoyed, some I didn't. I just didn't enjoy manga that were too sordid--I found them mentally fatiguing and hard too read. So I try to remember what I found interesting as a kid when drawing my own manga." Arakawa always tries to slip in a joke or two, even in prolonged, serious scenes. This stance appears to be in contrast to the heaviness of the anime version, which appeals to a very different taste.

See Glossary
Hiromu Arakawa
Shonen Gangan

See questions
01 03 05

05 Where does Arakawa get her ideas for the story?

According to Arakawa, the Philosopher's Stone was the starting point fro FMA. The Philosopher's Stone is also a very important item in the Square Enix game DragonQuest. Since Gangan was published by Square Enix, Arakawa figured that if she kept in mind the company's games, it would be easier for her to get her serial published. As a result, she made the Philosopher's Stone her point of departure. While researching the Philosopher's Stone, she kept bumping into the word "alchemy."

Alchemy was researched widely in medieval Europe. It attempted to find a way to turn the base metals into more valuable metals (particularly gold). It was believed that this could be done with a theoretical catalyst called the Philosopher's Stone. The idea for the Homunculus also came from alchemy. Paracelsus, an alchemist, is said to have created one. These legends regarding alchemy have become the core of her story. Arakawa's professed love for B-movies suggests she may have gotten further inspiration from films such as Frankenstein's Monster. The setting for the story resembles England during the Industrial Revolution. Alchemy seems to make a good match for an era when people are switching from using tools to machines.

See Glossary

Hiromu Arakawa
Philosopher's Stone
Alchemy
Alchemist
Homunculus

See questions
01 04 14 15

06 Where do the names Edward and Alphonse come from?

Edward's name was inspired by the Tim Burton film Edward Scissorhands (1990). His younger brother is named after the Comte Alphonse de Toulouse-Lautrec, father of the French artist Henri Marie Raymond de Toulouse-Lautrec Monfa. Their last name comes from the fantasy novel The Elric Saga.

S ee Glossary
Edward
Alphonse

Real Alchemists: 1
Nicholas Flamel

Because there actually was a practice called alchemy (it was for a time studied seriously, and was similar to chemistry), there were actual alchemists. Nicholas Flamel (1330-1410) was one such alchemist, and according to legend he managed to synthesize metals and create a Philosopher's Stone.

Originally a bookseller, Flamel apparently acquired a mysterious book written in Greek and Hebrew from which he learned about alchemy. It is said he learned a technique for producing gold, and was thus able to amass a fortune, much of which he used to assist churches, hospitals and charities. According to legend, he also succeeded in producing a Philosopher's Stone, giving him immortality.

Legends about Flamel's alchemy spread throughout the 17th and 18th centuries, but it was later judged that most of the texts on alchemy attributed to him were fakes. So, although Nicholas Flamel's existence has been verified, many of his alchemic feats are regarded as myth.

07 Why does Arakawa depict herself as a cow?

Hiromu Arakawa, FMA's creator, comes from an agricultural family in Hokkaido. She apparently is very fond of cows, having helped take care of them on her parent's farm. Furthermore, her Chinese zodiac sign is the Ox, and her astrological sign is Taurus. This amount of cow-connectedness probably explains why her self-portrait is that of a cow. Also, the first manga to influence Arakawa was Norakuro, a semi-autobiographical story by a veteran of the Japanese Imperial Army told through dogs. Maybe this approach of depicting oneself as an animal inspired her.

See Glossary
Hiromu Arakawa

See questions
04 08

The artist's real name is Hiromi Arakawa. She changed the final syllable (-mi) in her first name to create the alias Hiromu. In Japanese, names ending in the syllable "-mi" are often girls' names, while the character "Hiromu" is used for boys' names. As a result, for a long time many fans thought that FMA's creator was a man. When it was discovered that Hiromu is in fact a woman, it created a bit of a sensation. Arakawa commented, "I never meant to disguise my gender, nor did I ever say I was a man." Nevertheless, it seems pretty clear that she intended to write under a male pseudonym. This is not totally surprising, considering that there is still some bias against female authors in "shonen" (young adult/boy) manga. A few women, such as Rumiko Takahashi, have managed to succeed in the shonen manga genre, but for a newcomer like Arakawa, it must have seemed a bit daunting.

However some more astute readers guessed her gender from the manga itself. The women of the FMA series are all very independent. Also, there is a rich range of female characters in the series.

On the other hand, it has been observed that male artists tend to unconsciously depict women as in need of protection. In contrast to this, the female characters in FMA probably rescue the men as much as vice versa. Male manga artists also tend to draw generic female figures that conform to their ideal of feminine beauty. In FMA, however, the female characters are all individuals. These factors gave some of the sharper readers a clue as to Arakawa's gender.

For a long time, three elements (which happen to be the slogan of the famous Shonen Jump digest) were considered crucial to the success of a shonen manga: friendship, effort, and victory (probably because they are very easy concepts for the male artists to grasp). As a result, FMA projected a style and sensibility not found in shonen manga until then.

⑤ee Glossary
Hiromu Arakawa

See questions
04 07

09 What are the FMA games like?

The first FMA game was released in December 2003 by Gangan's parent company Square Enix a couple of months after the anime started. It is titled Fullmetal Alchemist and the Broken Angel and is available exclusively on PlayStation 2. The player controls Ed, and must use alchemy to defeat enemies. Fullmetal Alchemist 2: Curse of the Crimson Elixir, released September 2004, implements the same combat system, but features upgraded graphics and controls. The third title in the series, Fullmetal Alchemist 3: God of the Eternal Girl, has a two-player mode and allows the player to switch between Edward and Alphonse. Fullmetal Alchemist: Dream Carnival, released in 2004, is a fighting game featuring the FMA characters and including their signature techniques.

See Glossary

Shonen Gangan
Square Enix
Edward
Alphonse

See questions
03

part 02

Alchemy's Secrets

Alchemy was developed in medieval Europe for the purpose of turning base metals such as lead and iron into gold. Besides the production of gold, it aimed to perfect the human spirit (in other words allow people to become closer to God or become one with God). Alchemy also included the study of turning inanimate matter into living creatures, for example creating artificial miniature humans called homunculi. Alchemy is an Arabic word, and it is thought the practice was spread to Europe by the growth of Islam. However, research into transforming one substance into another began in ancient Egypt, and was studied in ancient Greece by Aristotle. Alchemy as studied in Greece was transmitted to Islam, and was first researched in Europe in 1144, when "Liber de compositione alchimiae," an Arabic text on alchemy, was translated into Latin. In some respects alchemy is very similar to modern sciences (for example, the combining of hydrogen and oxygen to make water). However, the modern chemical principles of atoms and molecules were not understood. As a result, people studied under the belief that they could truly turn iron into gold. It was also believed that living things, such as humans, could be created through alchemy once techniques had developed sufficiently. Alchemy also probably included those who understood it as a kind of magic, and there were undoubtedly fraudulent alchemy scholars. Fullmetal Alchemist introduces such a character in the person of Father Cornello.

In the world of Fullmetal Alchemist, alchemy seems to be a sort of science. The alchemists, such as the Elric brothers, research the physical compositions of everything in their world, decompose them at the atomic level, then reconstruct them in new forms. During this process, the most important concept is the "Law of Equivalent Exchange," a principle that is important in chemical formulas even in modern science. This rule is also called the "Law of Conservation of Energy," and states that when one substance is changed into another, the total amount of energy, including head energy created by the process, must be exactly the same before and after. In other words, the alchemists in the story all understand the basic natural rule that you can't make something out of nothing.

See Glossary

Alchemy
Homunculi
Father Cornello
Elric Brothers
Alchemist

See questions

11

11   What does the concept of "one is all, all is one" have to do with alchemy?

Edward and Alphonse decide to study under Izumi Curtis to improve their alchemy abilities. She requires them to pass a test before she will accept them as her pupils. For the test, she takes them to the deserted Yock Island in the middle of Kauroy Lake, and forces them to survive their for one month. Through this experience they naturally come to understand the principle of "one is all, all is one." It can be rephrased "the world is the all, and I am the one." This concept comes from Zen Buddhism, and appears to have little to do with alchemy, but the idea that "one is all, all is one" can in fact be traced back to alchemy. Alchemy states that all matter in the world is created by God, and is originally a single substance. This becomes divided to form the differentiated things seen in the world. This can be understood in terms of physics--cosmologists have theorized that originally everything in the universe was compressed into a single point in spacetime, causing the Big Bang that created our universe. The natural sciences have also shown that "one can influence all". For example, even lowly bugs are important to the ecology, especially to the birds that eat them. Alchemy combines chemistry, physics and natural science. Alchemists decompose and reconstruct matter, and this has an overall impact on the world as a whole. Izumi Curtis follows the "Law of Natural Providence," which dictates that things created through alchemic transmutation are part of the natural world, and she hopes that by observing nature the Elric brothers will come to understand this.

See Glossary

Edward
Alphose
Izumi Curtis
Alchemy
Yock Island
Kauroy Lake
Elric Brothers

See questions

11 **43**

12 Are "transmutation circles" needed to perform alchemy?

In order to perform alchemic techniques, the alchemist must understand the composition of the substance, decompose it, then reconstruct it. Special circles, called transmutation circles, are required for the decomposing and reconstruction steps. These circles must always have a central point, into which power is focused from the circumference. The circle also represents the revolution of time.

Formula are written around the circle. These describe the composition of the substance, and the transmutation process-- they're similar to chemical formula. The object to be transmuted is placed in the center of the circle. The alchemist then activates it with her energy (or "ki") and the object is transmuted into the new object. The fact that each alchemist has a different style of transmutation circle and their secretiveness indicates that alchemy is a very solitary study, with each alchemist doing their own research and development. For example, they encode or try to hide the results of their research. (Edward keeps his research results in a "travel diary," while Dr. Marcoh keeps his written in a "recipe book.") Truly great alchemists can perform alchemy with simple transmutation circles and formula.

See Glossary
Transmutation circles
Alchemy
Alchemist
Formula

13 Why are there various kinds of alchemists?

J ust within the State Alchemists one can find a variety of titles, including the Fullmetal Alchemist, Flame Alchemist, Sewing Life Alchemist, Strong Arm Alchemist, etc. This likely indicates that the alchemists are more like scientists than magicians. Just as the sciences have physicists, archaeologists, geologists, cosmologists, and so on, alchemists too specialize in the stage of alchemy--understanding, decomposition, or reconstruction-- with the material that they are best at using (metal, stone, etc.). Edward, who is famous as a prodigy in the field of alchemy, is adept at using a variety of substances but, as his title implies, seems best at transmuting metals.

See Glossary

Alchemist
State Alchemists
Fullmetal Alchemist
Flame Alchemist
Sewing Life Alchemist
Strong Alchemist

See questions
16

Real Alchemists: 2
Paracelsus

Paracelsus (1493-1541) was a famous alchemist of the 15th century. His actual name was Phillip von Hohenheim, and in Fullmetal Alchemist, he seems to be the model for the Elric Brothers' father, also called von Hohenheim. Paracelsus originally trained as a doctor, entering the University of Basel in 1525, but later became a wandering physician after he was expelled for criticizing Christianity. He later studied alchemy, and is said to have succeeded in creating a homunculus.

However, this is probably a legend based on his reputation for criticizing Christianity (i.e. he actually flaunted God by creating life himself), and his books, in which he cited philosophy, astrology and alchemy as the basis for medicine. The name Paracelsus itself means "greater than Celsus," in reference to a famous physician of ancient Rome. Although Paracelsus was indeed a great physician, the story about the homunculus is, of course, apocryphal and probably results from his status as "legendary alchemist."

14 What is the Philosopher's Stone?

A concept that appeared in alchemic studies in medieval Europe. It was a theoretical catalyst that could turn base metals like lead into gold. It was also called the Celestial Stone, or Fifth Element. In their search for the Philosopher's Stone, researchers in the middle ages analyzed various substances, and as a result alchemy developed into chemistry. In the middle ages, people believed that mercury was the substance closest to the Philosopher's Stone. Since it is both a liquid and a metal, it was thought to hold important clues on how to change substances. It was thought that the Philosopher's Stone could be produced by adding some unknown substance to mercury. In FMA, the Philosopher's Stone is a substance that allows alchemists to overcome the Law of Equivalent Exchange. Using this stone, not only could one create something out of nothing, it would give the possessor the power to overcome death itself, becoming immortal. It's base is a liquid substance, perhaps similar to mercury. By adding enough human souls, it becomes a Philosopher's Stone. Therefore, the Philosopher's Stone does not actually make something out of nothing. It uses the power stored in many human souls, so the Law of Equivalent Exchange is not violated. Of course, the idea that the unknown substances needed to make the Philosopher's Stone are human souls was author Arakawa's original idea.

See Glossary
Philosopher's Stone

See questions
05 15

15 How can the Philosopher's Stone make something out of nothing?

U sing a Philosopher's Stone, an alchemist can overcome the Law of Equivalent Exchange, for example, turn a small amount of matter into something much larger. When Edward fails to bring his mother back, he realizes that he needs something that will let him break the Law of Equivalent Exchange to perform the human transmutation. That something, he assumes, is the Philosopher's Stone, and this is how he becomes interested in the stone. Because the Philosopher's Stone is created by sacrificing many lives, whenever it is used to perform a transmutation, it is the equivalent of using human life to make an equivalent exchange. Therefore, the Philosopher's Stone in no way creates something out of nothing; the Law of Equivalent Exchange is not broken. The Philosopher's Stone is small though, so it appears to create things out of thin air.

See Glossary
Philosopher's Stone

See questions
05 14

"**A**lchemists are for the people."
Ideally, these words are etched
into the heart of every alchemist.
While they are like scientists, the use of
alchemy can give them great power too. In
Edward's era, just like in our world today,
each country has a military for "self
defense." Because the military of Amestris
seeks power, it is probably natural that they
show favor to the alchemists. In our real
world too, scientists, who are crucial to
developing nuclear weapons, missiles, and so
on, are often given special favors (such as
research grants and scholarships) by their
own governments. However, if these
"alchemists" become too cozy with their
governments and military, the state's authority may become too oligarchic, leading to a
dictatorship in which the needs of the people
are not given priority. The motto "alchemists
are for the people" is meant to remind the
alchemists of which goals they should use

their exceptional talents for. Edward sees the State Alchemist system as a shortcut to finding a way to reunite the spirit and body of his brother Alphonse. Edward is in fact one of the more favored State Alchemists, and is allowed to conduct research on the Philosopher's Stone at his own discretion. However, even though he knows that, theoretically, if a war breaks out, there's a danger that he'll be called on to use his alchemy skills as a weapon, he doesn't seem to really believe this will happen. After all, at the beginning of the story, he's still young and has a limited perspective on things. As the story progresses, he comes to understand how truly dangerous alchemy can be. He also discovers that his country's political and military leader, Fuhrer Bradley, is really a Homunculus. Given this, the government's purpose for catering to the alchemists may have other implications.

See Glossary

Alchemist
Alchemy
Edward
State Alchemist
Philosopher's Stone
King Bradley
Homunculus

See questions
13

17 What's needed to perform a human transmutation?

It seems that at least three elements are needed to transmute a human: flesh, will, and soul. The flesh is physical, so its composition can be understood through analysis. The soul not only controls the flesh, but is the source of emotions and memories. The will is what binds the flesh and soul together. When the Elric brothers attempt to resurrect their mother, they have an understanding of the principles behind the flesh and the soul, but not the will. Because of this, their transmutation attempt fails. They mistakenly believe that they are missing a Philosopher's Stone, and this is why the human transmutation failed, when in fact what they needed was Truth. In short, alchemists, such as Edward, simply do not have a perfect understanding of the relationship between flesh, soul and will. The compositional elements of soul and will are theoretical to begin with. That is, the crucial element for human transmutation is Truth.

In fact, there are historical legends about alchemists who have created artificial humans called Homunculi. The legends say that Homunculi could be produced by filling a flask with human semen and herbs and letting it sit in warm, fermenting horse dung. After 14 days, a translucent human figure would form. This would grow into a Homunculus if given human blood and kept warm for another 14 weeks. It required fresh blood everyday. The growing Homunculus would soon die if removed from the flask or if its blood supply was cut off. On reaching maturity, it would resemble a human child, but be much smaller than a real human. Homunculi were said to be born with an innate knowledge of various thing.

S ee Glossary

Human transmutation
Elric brothers
Philosopher's Stone
Edward
Homunculi

See questions
60

Real Alchemists: 3
Alessandro di Cagliostro

Alessandro di Cagliostro (1743-1795) was a con artist who claimed to be an alchemist. He gained great wealth by claiming to be a disciple of the Greek alchemist Althotas (a person whose existence is unverifiable), and selling his services to the aristocracy. However, he was later arrested in connection with the "affair of the diamond necklace" (in which an expensive necklace was fraudulently ordered on behalf of Marie Antoinette and stolen), and was eventually exiled. He was arrested for heresy in Rome in 1789, and died in prison in 1795.

There were in fact many charlatans claiming to be alchemists in Europe during the 18th century, but Cagliostro was probably the most famous.

18 *What is this "Truth" that Edward and Izumi see in the Gate?*

Although the "Truth" depicted in FMA has a number of very deep, philosophical implications, it can be summed up as the "Answer." The Homunculus notwithstanding, no one knows the "Answer" to the question of how to perform human transmutation. Only those who have the "Answer," or see the "Truth" have a shot at successfull human transmutation.

The Elric brothers and Izumi Curtis both try human transmutation, losing parts of their body (or in Alphonse's case, his whole body) in the process. This is called "rebound" and occurs when an alchemist attempts a transmutation beyond her own knowledge and skill. To satisfy the Law of Equivalent Exchange, part of the alchemist's flesh is exchanged. Edward and Izumi try to perform human transmutations and fail, but are given a glimpse of the Truth in exchange for parts of their bodies. If they are shown the Truth, one would think they'd then be able to perform a human transmutation, but this is not the case. It turns out that the Truth is that human transmutation is impossible. In fact, in Edward's world, human transmutation is considered unnatural and is taboo. This has nothing to do with religious reasons. If it did, research such as Shou Tucker's human/animal chimeras would probably also be taboo. The reason human transmutation is taboo probably has to do with the fact that the cost is very high, as seen when Edward and Izumi try it. Previous alchemists must have realized that it was dangerous and in any case impossible, and this is why it's taboo. The closest thing to a transmuted human in the manga are the Homunculi. Has Father, the character who created the Homunculi, seen the Truth? This is not yet known.

See Glossary

Truth
Homunculus
Erlic broyhers
Izumi Curtis
Alphonse
Shou Tucker

See questions
19

19 Why is Edward able to perform alchemy without a transmutation circle?

According to Izumi, Edward is able to perform transmutations without a transmutation circle because he glimpsed the Truth during his attempted human transmutation. She knows this because she too tried to perform a human transmutation to bring back her dead child. She too saw the Truth and was then able to perform alchemy without a transmutation circle. In the scene in which Edward sees the Truth, it is rendered abstractly. He said it felt as if large amounts of information had suddenly drilled into his head, so the secret of how to perform alchemy without a transmutation circle must have been part of this information.

What other information Edward may have learned is not described in the story, but it seems clear that Edward makes a circle with his arms, pressing his palms together. This seems to serve the same function as a transmutation circle. By recalling the correct formula in his head, he can mentally "write" it to the circle formed with his body. In other words, Edward is his own transmutation circle. If what Edward and Izumi saw in the circle is supposed to be the Truth, it would seem that originally alchemy was meant to be performed without a transmutation circle.

See Glossary

Izumi Curtis
Edward
Human transmutation
Transmutation circle

See questions
12 18

20 How is the Rentan Jutsu developed in Xing different from alchemy?

Xing is a country lying far east of Amestris and separated from it by a desert. This country seems to be modeled on China. Rentan Jutsu was actually a form of alchemy researched in ancient China. It focused on finding an elixir of immortality called Grand Elixir of Immortality. In addition to long life, the elixir was said to bestow the wisdom of a sage. The search for the elixir led to the development of various Chinese medicines. Just as alchemy was related to chemistry and physics, Rentan Jutsu was related to the study of pharmacology and medicine. In FMA, Mei Chan and Ling Yao leave their home to search for the secret to immortality in Amestris. This actually is a direct reference to the historical figure Shi Huangdi, an ancient Chinese king of the Qin state. He is said to have sent his family to various places in search of the secret to immortality. At that time in China, mercury was considered to be the most promising ingredient for an elixir to eternal life. Ironically, Shi Huangdi ingested mercury to try to prolong his life, but this probably actually shortened it. The character Father, who creates the Homunculi, is able to neutralize Edward's alchemy, but Mei Chan's Rentan Jutsu techniques still work normally. From this, it is apparent that alchemy and Rentan Jutsu work via a different mechanism.

See Glossary

Rentan Jutsu
Xing
Alchemy
Mei Chan
Ling Yao
Father
Edward

See questions
21

part 03

FMA World's
Secrets

21 | *When did alchemic research begin in Amestris.*

I n the distant past, Amestris (the country Edward and Alphonse call home) produced a number of primitive forms of alchemy, but they were largely theoretical and not very useful. The true beginning of alchemy was in the desert nation of Xerxes, some hundreds of years prior to the FMA story arc. It is said that a solitary philosopher appeared there one day, bringing the techniques with him. Also, the eastern country of Xing had techniques similar to alchemy called Rentan Jutsu. Since this art too arose hundreds of years ago, it's speculated that it may have been introduced by the same philosopher. The philosopher's name isn't known in either country, so this may be just a legend.

However, in the middle of the desert, in the ruins of Xerxes, there is a wall still bearing a mural depicting some sort of magical army, possibly a vestige of the philosopher's legacy. There is a similar design in

Laboratory 5 where the military conducts research on Philosopher's Stones. Given that some of the Homunculi, like Lust, are hundreds of years old, some fans speculate that the Homunculi creator, Father (appears in the manga only), might be this philosopher from Xerxes.

See questions
20 22

22 Why is Amestris under military rule?

Amestris is a country composed of many ethnicities. Perhaps the military itself arose in the past to suppress frequent violence between the various clans. The establishment of the current government, in which the military controls every aspect of the political system, seems to have been brought about by the incumbent president, King Bradley. He ascended to the top of the military in his 40s, after which he created the State Alchemist system. This served to concentrate political power with the central government, and through military intervention in other countries and suppression of domestic uprisings, the military became involved in politics, allowing Bradley to become the government's highest authority.

However, King Bradley's true form is that of a Homunculus (Wrath in the manga, Pride in the anime) and his true loyalty lies with the one who created him (Father in the manga, Dante in the anime).

Thus, it was this shadow ruler who is ultimately responsible for turning Amestris into a military state to further his/her own ends. As a country ruled by its military, Amestris is an aggressive nation and prone to starting wars. During these wars many lives are sacrificed, but it's these lives that are indispensable to creating Philosopher's Stones. In other words, Amestris' shadow ruler needed to turn the country into a military state in order to start wars and sacrifice huge numbers of lives.

See Glossary

Amestris
King Bradley
State Alchemist
Wrath
Pride
Father
Dante
Philosopher's Stone

See questions
21 **65** **67**

23 How is Amestris' military organized?

Amestris is ruled by a completely centralized government. The government is located mainly in Central City. Also located in Central are the Alchemy Research Center, library and military headquarters. Promotion to a station in Central is an honor reserved for the elite and this is the main motivation for the rank and file. Every part of the country is under direct control by the military by means of command centers which administer the citizens. In terms of military hierarchy, the privates are organized under corporals and form the base of the command pyramid. The other ranks, from low to high, are: Sergeant, Master Sergeant, Warrant Officer, Second Lieutenant, First Lieutenant, Captain, Major, Lieutenant Colonel, Colonel, Brigadier General, Major General, Lieutenant General, General, Fuhrer.

S ee Glossary
Amestris
Central City

See questions
22

24 Do Amestris and Xing (the country east of it) have different political systems?

While Amestris is a military state, a democratic framework is under construction. In contrast, Xing is ruled by a hereditary emperor who administers the country. When the emperor dies, the next heir in line succeeds the throne. This is rather complicated as Xing is a diverse country containing over 50 clans. To keep things fair, each clan sends the emperor a princess consort by which he produces children. As a result, there can be over 50 heirs to the throne at any given time. Of course, this spawns fierce arguments whenever a new emperor must be selected. This state of affairs leads Ling Yao, next in line for the throne, to seek a Philosopher's Stone in order to obtain immortality. Becoming an immortal emperor would greatly affect the fortunes of the 500,000 members of his clan (the Yao clan).

See Glossary
Amestris
Xing
Ling Yao
Philosopher's Stone

See questions
20 **21**

Y ouswell is the heart of industry and coal production in Amestris and most of its citizens are miners. The town is administered by Yoki, a lieutenant who earned his rank by virtue of paying off the Central officials. He exploits the town's people, cutting the miners' wages. Everyone hates Yoki's methods, but since he is a soldier, no one dares oppose him. The citizens have no respect for a military in which people like Yoki can simply buy their rank, and by extension they object to their government's way of doing things. On learning Edward is a State Alchemist, the townspeople treat him coldly. Not only do they regard him as being with the government (which they regard as the people's enemy), they assume he is not carrying out his duty as an alchemist to work for the common citizens.

Although normally both the military and National Alchemists work for the people, the citizens of Youswell have suffered so long under Yoki, they have come to oppose anything associated with the government.

See Glossary
Youswell
Amestris
Yoki
Edward
State Alchemist

Ishbal is an area located in the inhospitable eastern region of Amestris. The people of this country are physically distinct and have a religion and history that predates Amestris. They worship a god named Ishbala. According to their doctrine, "we and everything in our world are connected to Ishbala." The laws of nature themselves are regarded as exulted by god. Therefore, research seen as violating natural laws, such as alchemy, is rejected. This stance has lead to a longstanding debate between Ishbal and Amestris. However this turns into a war, one of the largest in Amestris' history, due to a certain event. Amestris makes liberal use of State Alchemists during this conflict, which becomes known as the Ishbal Rebellion. As a result, the people of Ishbal are all but annihilated, and Ishbal is annexed by Amestris.

The event that triggered this full-scale war was the ostensibly accidental slaying of an Ishbalan child by an Amestris soldier. At first blush, this incident seems to have been engineered by the Amestris army to provide an excuse for a land grab. However, given that the Homunculus Envy admits that it was he, disguised as one of the moderate (i.e. anti-war) soldiers, who killed the child, it is obvious that this was the will of Father. Apparently, Father created a Philosopher's Stone from the souls of the many Ishbalans who were killed during the war. It is also likely that Father carried out the one-night destruction of Xerxes. He sees Amestris as a training ground, for which he has some very large plans, but what those might be is as of yet unclear. In the anime, the Father character doesn't exist, although Dante plays a similar role. She does not create the Homunculi herself, and is motivated by the personal desire to acquire a complete Philosopher's Stone and use it to gain eternal life.

See Glossary

Ishbal
Amestris
Ishbala
Alchemy
Statel Alchemist
Ishbal Rebellion
Homunculus
Envy
Father
Philosopher's Stone
Xerxes
Dante

See questions
20 27

Real Alchemists: 4
Comte de Saint-Germain

The Count of St Germain (d. 1784) is the most mysterious of the historical alchemists. He suddenly appeared in the French court during the 18th century and ingratiated himself with the royal family. He claimed to be 4,000 years old (according to French records, he was a man of around 50 in 1710, and 25 years later was described as being about 25 when he appeared in the Netherlands; his age seemed to fluctuate depending on the writer). Even after his death, there were reports of sightings of him from around Europe. From the reports and eyewitness accounts, he has gained a reputation for being an alchemist that has attained true immortality through his techniques. There is even a legend that he instructed Cagliostro.

It is widely thought that there have in fact been several people using the name Comte de Saint-Germain to commit fraud in the past, thus explaining the different accounts of his appearance.

27 Why does Risembool have such advanced automail technology?

R isembool, hometown of the Elric brothers, is known for its highly developed automail. The town was originally home to many makers of prosthetics. During the Ishbal Rebellion, there was an increase in the number of people who had lost limbs, so the demand for well-made artificial limbs spiked. As a result, automail, which was developed using alchemy, became highly valued, leading Risembool to expand into the automail business. The town is home to many excellent automail makers including Edward's childhood friend Winry. Compared with the eastern country of Xing, which possesses highly developed medical techniques called Rentan Jutsu, Amestris' alchemy is closer to chemistry, and its medical uses are not very advanced. This may be another reason why automail is so highly valued, and why it has been developed.

S ee Glossary

Risembool
Elric Brothers
Automail
Ishbal Rebellion
Alchemy
Edward
Winry
Xing
Rentan Jutsu
Amestris

See questions
20 26

28 How does Edward move his artificial limbs?

Normally, prosthetic limbs cannot move themselves, but when automail is connected directly to the user's nervous system, prosthetic limbs can be moved freely right down to the fingertips. However, because automail is hooked up to the nervous system, the user feels great pain when first putting it on. Sometimes the pain is so great the user actually dies. Even if the user is able to successfully wear the automail, it takes a lot of practice before it can be used as freely as the user's natural limbs. Edward repeatedly damages his automail, and it causes him hellish pain every time Winry fits him with new mail.

See Glossary
Edward
Automail
Winry

E dward sees becoming a State Alchemist as a shortcut in his research on Philosopher's Stones and a step toward learning the Truth. Furthermore, in the Amestris military, alchemists are given preferential treatment, and joining the State Alchemists gives alchemists access to past alchemic research and government funding, allowing them to carry out even more advanced research. There is also a financial incentive to join. State Alchemists receive a silver clock and an official title.

The test to become a State Alchemist consists of four parts--written test, skill test, psychological evaluation, and interview. It's a very tough test, and so far only 200 people have passed. Although a hard profession to break into, the pros of becoming a State Alchemist are great. However, the job comes with cons too.

Becoming a State Alchemist is tantamount to entering the military. State Alchemists must fight as soldiers in places where conflicts arise, and are not permitted to refuse use of their alchemic techniques to the military. The general public refers to State Alchemists disparagingly as "army dogs," as their alchemic techniques are used as little more than weapons of mass destruction.

S ee Glossary

Edward
Statel Alchemist
Amestris

See questions

22 **30**

30 | Are State Alchemists periodically tested?

E ven if an alchemist passes the exam, they're still not out of the woods. They are subject to review once a year, and they must report on the progress of their research. They must do this because, as State Alchemists, they are expected to constantly contribute to the field of alchemy. Those who are not enthusiastic about research, and cannot contribute to the military have their State Alchemist license revoked. Shou Tucker turns his own daughter into a chimera for the alchemist's review. This indicates that the alchemist review is extremely tough; not only did Tucker use his own daughter, but this sort of act is actually forbidden, suggesting that the review is so hard that people must resort to illegal techniques.

S ee Glossary
State Alchemist
Alchemy
Shou Tucer

See questions
29

Human transmutation is forbidden, both for moral and legal reasons. State Alchemists who are found practicing human transmutation are immediately stripped of their rank. This is ironic, since the military's leader (the Fuhrer) is actually a transmuted human. Either way, since human transmutation is forbidden, regardless of whether it succeeds or fails, it would appear that Edward, who tried to transmute his mother, has no right to become a State Alchemist.

Strangely, it was Mustang who recommended Edward become a State Alchemist, despite knowing about Ed's attempt at transmutation. Mustang's reason for encouraging this breach of the rules was perhaps twofold. He must have been impressed that the young brothers had the ability to perform a human transmutation, but he probably also felt sympathetic for them, as they ended up losing their own flesh and limbs in the process.

Mustang likely considered becoming State Alchemists a quick way for the brothers to learn the techniques needed to restore their lost flesh. Since performing human transmutation makes one ineligible to become a State Alchemist, Mustang keeps Edward's attempt a secret from the military. If their transgression was revealed, Edward would lose his job instantly. On the other hand, Father wants to use Edward as a human sacrifice to open the Gate, and therefore works behind the scenes to put him in the military and thus within his reach. As a result, even if Edward's attempt at human transmutation became publicly known, he would probably not lose his position.

See Glossary

State Alchemist
Human transmutation
Roy Mustang
Father
Gate

See questions
32

After it's revealed that the government is performing Philosopher's Stone research at Laboratory 5 in Central City, it becomes apparent that part of the military have participated in human transmutation experiments. It's then revealed that the Fuhrer, who heads the military, is in fact a Homunculus. We further learn that Father creates the Homunculi from his own body. These Homunculi cannot strictly be called "human." They appear to be human, but aren't. Father tries to use Edward and Mustang as human sacrifices to open the Gate. Looking at the story up until now, it seems that while the military can make things that appear to be human, they cannot produce real humans. In the anime, Homunculi are created during failed attempts at human transmutation, and at first do not have human form. By feeding on incomplete Philosopher's Stones, called Red Stones (anime only), they can take on human form.

In general, these Homunculi are motivated by their desire to become human. In the anime, no one has ever performed a perfect human transmutation.

ee Glossary

Human transmutation
Philosopher's Stone
Faher
Homunculi
Roy Mustang
Red Stone

See questions
31

33 What is on the other side of the Gate?

The Gate is handled differently in the manga and anime. In the anime, there seems to be another world (the real world) on the other side of the Gate. In one world, alchemy can be used, in the other world it cannot. The world where alchemy does not exist is our "real" world. Meanwhile, Edward and the other alchemists live in a parallel world, where they use the souls of people who die in our world to power their techniques. In other words, according to the anime version, alchemy uses the souls of the dead whether or not a Philosopher's Stone is involved. The formula for alchemy is base object + souls from parallel world = new object. Thus, the Law of Equivalent Exchange (conservation of matter/energy) never really existed to begin with.

In contrast, the story in the manga is still unfolding, and it isn't clear what is on the other side of the Gate. Considering that the "false Gate" created by Father inside

Gluttony was used by Edward to return from the "void" in Gluttony's stomach to the real world, it appears likely that the Gate connects with a different world. As of now, all that's known is that the Truth is said to lie on the other side of the Gate.

See Glossary

Gate
Edward
Philosopher's Stone
Formula
Father
Gluttony

See questions
18 **62**

part 04

Character's Secrets

34 Why did Edward stop growing at 12?

S ee Glossary
Edward

Edward is currently 15 years old, but at 150 cm is quite short for his age. Even with his boots and spiky hair, he's only about 165 cm. As a result, he's often called "shorty," "bean boy," and other pejoratives, sometimes provoking him to pummel his tormentors. His height is a running gag throughout the story. His short stature is probably not just a genetic problem and throughout the story various explanations are offered. Perhaps his heavy automail is stunting his growth. Or maybe during his human transmutation attempt, not only his arm and leg, but also his ability to grow were taken from him. It may even be because he and his brother Alphonse have a physical bond. The true reason is unknown.

35 Why can Edward perform alchemy even before he's had any training?

When Edward was young, his father, an alchemist named Van Hohenheim, left home. However, he left his books, which Edward read, allowing him to master the art of alchemy. In other words, he's a self-taught alchemist. He has an incredible ability to concentrate on things that interest him. The way he pours over documents in Shou Tucker's home, and decodes the encoded notes left by Marcoh give some hint as to his concentration ability. There is little doubt that he has a sharp mind. However, mere intelligence does not a great alchemist make. The amount of "ki", or mental energy, possessed by the alchemist greatly influences how powerful he/she is. Edward is very strong in this department too. He probably inherited this trait from his father. In short, Edward learned about alchemy through a combination of natural talent and the documents left by his father.

See Glossary
Edward
Alchemy
Hohenheim
Shou Tacker
Dr. Marcoh

36 Ed's title is the "Fullmetal Alchemist." Is this because he specializes in transmuting metals?

State Alchemists receive a "second name," and Ed's is the Fullmetal Alchemist. This is not because he specializes in alchemy involving metal. Rather, the name comes from his automail limbs. As can be seen from the titles of the various State Alchemists, their titles don't necessarily describe the techniques they use. While Mustang's title, the Flame Alchemist, is due to the fact that he's adept at fire techniques, Basque Grand is dubbed the Iron Blood Alchemist due to his motto. Even so, Edward does seem pretty good at transmuting metals. For example, during his StateAlchemist exam, he transmutes a spear. Therefore his title is doubly fitting--it matches both his appearance and his style of alchemy.

See Glossary

Edward
Fullmetal Alchemist
State Alchemist
Roy Mustang
Flame Alchemist
Basque Grand
Iron Blood Alchemist

37 Why is Edward such a good martial artist?

Edward has mastered powerful martial art techniques that he uses in battles. These he learned from his mentor Izumi Curtis. She firmly believed that strengthening the mind required strengthening the body, and she used martial arts, which require one to read one's opponent's moves, to teach him the principals of alchemy. As a result, Edward becomes a strong fighter. Although a State Alchemist, ironically Edward makes a pretty good soldier too. In fact, many State Alchemists are highly skilled warriors--Mustang and Armstrong come to mind. These alchemists have trained their bodies in order to harness the enormous energies required for their techniques, and as a result have become excellent warriors. In this sense, many alchemists are probably innately suited to military service.

See Glossary
Edward
Izumi Curtis
State Alchemist
Roy Mustang
Armstrong

Alphonse lost his body while trying to perform a human transmutation, a very high level alchemy technique which requires a trade-off to satisfy the Law of Equivalent Exchange. Edward gives up his arm and leg in exchange for bringing Alphonse's soul back. Why does Alphonse lose his body? It was Edward, after all, who performed the human transmutation. Alphonse was just helping. Actually, this had nothing to do with the trade-off required by the alchemy; it was a simple accident. It's thought that Alphonse's body is on the other side of the Gate in the "real" world. In fact, Edward glimpses him through a crevice in the Gate. However, it is unclear whether it is actually Alphonse's body, or the mental picture of Alphonse as remembered by Edward.

Therefore, as of this point in the manga series, it isn't known exactly where Alphonse's body is. Furthermore, even if Alphonse's flesh body does still exist somewhere, without a soul it is the equivalent of a corpse, and is probably rotting... In the anime, Ed resurrects Al, who revives in his 10 year-old body with no memory of events since their attempt at performing a human transmutation. Also in the anime, the Gate is the door to a parallel world. Alphonse's body continues to exist in this world.

🅢ee Glossary

Alphonse
Human Transmutation
Edward
Gate

39 How is Alphonse able to talk?

Alphonse existence, if you can call it that, is as a soul connected to a suit of armor. As a suit of armor, he cannot feel pain, eat or sleep. So it seems strange that he can talk despite having no mouth.

It's possible that Alphonse is not literally speaking, but rather is using some sort of telepathy to communicate his thoughts to others. Alphonse's existence is not actually physical (the armor is just a vessel that keeps his soul anchored). He is probably not capable of producing sound (which is the physical vibration of air) but rather communicates his thoughts directly to the hearts of others.

See Glossary
Alphonse

40 Is Alphonse's alchemy weaker than his brother's?

A s a State Alchemist, Edward is known as a prodigy and his abilities are highly praised both in the military and among common people. By comparison, Alphonse's skills seem good, but nowhere near his brother's. Alphonse is also a year younger than Edward. So it seems that Edward's alchemy skills are more developed than Alphonse's. On the other hand, like Edward, from his glimpse into the Truth, he became able to perform alchemy without a transmutation circle.

He cannot take the State Alchemist exam anyway, because it requires a physical check, which is impossible for Alphonse. Besides, part of the praise Edward gets is probably due to the authority given him by his position as State Alchemist. The actual gap in abilities between the two brothers probably isn't that large.

See Glossary

State Alchemist
Alphonse
Edward
Transmutation Circle

41 Why does Winry love machines so much?

Winry's parents were doctors, and she was originally interested in medicine. However, when she was eight, her parents died in the Ishbal Rebellion. Afterwards, her grandmother Pinako raises her. Pinako is an automail mechanic, and this seems to have influenced Winry.

She is sometimes chided for being a bit obsessive about her interest, but part of her enthusiasm probably stems from her desire to create ever better automail for Edward. For his part, Edward seems to want no one other than Winry to work on his automail--he returns to Risembool for repairs and installation, and sometimes calls Winry into the field when he needs maintenance. Also, as the daughter of doctors, Winry wants to develop quality automail in order to allow people with disabilities to move freely--she's not just an automail "otaku."

ee Glossary

Winry
Ishbal Rebellion
Pinako
Automail
Edward
Risembool

See questions
27

42 Is it true that Winry is less popular in the anime than in the manga?

In the manga, Edward is quite emotional and sometimes laughs uncontrollably, but in the anime his character has a cooler personality. Therefore, Winry inherits this tendency to laugh excessively. As a result of this and her tendency to say extreme things, fans of the character in the manga didn't enjoy her anime appearances as much.

In the manga and anime, the characters and story details are different, but Winry is the most well-known example of a character that brings out fans' preference for either the manga or the anime.

See Glossary
Winry
Edward

43 Why isn't Izumi Curtis more widely known?

Besides being the Elric brothers' mentor, Izumi is an alchemist of considerable talent. However, she has a policy of not accepting pupils and tries not to use alchemy. She definitely does not bill herself as a great alchemist. As a result, she hasn't gained a lot of fame.

At the age of 18, she went to study under Gold Steiner, who made her survive on Briggs Mountain with just a knife for one month. During this experience she internalized the alchemic concept of "one is all, all is one," which began her career. Given that alchemy emphasizes spirituality over convenience, and that Izumi tried to resurrect her own child with a forbidden human transmutation, maybe she doubted her own suitability as an instructor of alchemy. This is why she decided to use alchemy as little as possible.

In the anime, Izumi's instructor is Dante, creator of the Homunculi. It is hard to think that Dante, who is motivated by personal gain, taught Izumi the spiritual concept of "one is all, all is one." While Dante recognizes Izumi's talents, she disdains humans and probably didn't understand Izumi's stoicism.

See Glossary

Izimi Curtis
Elric Brothers
Alchemy
Dante
Homunculi

See questions

44

Hiromu Arakawa, the artist herself, has said that when she first thought up the character Izumi, she wanted to show her saying, "I'm a part-time housewife!" She helps operate the butcher's shop, and is both strict and kind. She is totally in love with her husband Sig. Sadly, this love is related to her attempt at performing a human transmutation on her stillborn son, during which she lost a number of internal organs. As a result she can no longer have children and suffers from a frail constitution and occasional bouts of coughing up blood. Izumi seems more proud of her husband Sig than of her alchemy skills. Perhaps Hiromu Arakawa wanted to use Izumi as an antithesis to the normal image of alchemy in her story, in which it is often associated with great or powerful characters.

Izumi demonstrates that whether housewife or alchemist, we all are just puny humans who sometimes make mistakes. In the anime, a Homunculus (Wrath) is born from her attempt at performing a human transmutation, she has a relationship with Dante, and is a rather severe character. In the manga, she is a more cheerful character despite her coughing fits.

See Glossary

Hiromu Arakawa
Izumi Curtis
Sig
Homunculus
Wrath
Human transmutation
Dante

See questions
43

45 *What sort of person is Hohenheim?*

Whe the anime began, the character Hohenheim still had not
appeared in the manga. He's the
Elric brothers' father, and is called
"Hohenheim of Light." He has lived about
400 years by moving his soul between various host bodies, as has Dante. However, his
body is beginning to decay, albeit at a slower
rate than Dante's (it seems that when changing bodies, he ages slightly). Trying to reason with Dante, he is pushed through the
Gate into the "real" world.

In the manga too, Hohenheim never seems to
age and doesn't die even if shot. He does not
seem fully human, but on learning of Trisha's
(his wife) death, he is truly sad. He also
regards Edward and Alphonse fondly, and
does indeed love his family. He seems kind
of spaced out, so its hard to tell what he's
thinking. He seems to know of some great
event yet in store. He also looks somewhat
like and seems to be acquainted with Father,

the mysterious figure who lives underground and is the creator of the Homunculi in the manga. He is undoubtedly a key character to the story.

S ee Glossary
Hoenheim
Elric brothers
Dante
Trisha
Edward
Alphonse
Homunculi

See questions
46

46 Why is Pinako surprised that Hohenheim hasn't changed?

Pinako has known Hohenheim since before the Elric brothers were born, and was close to him until he suddenly left home. Pinako is an intelligent woman, and picked up on the fact that there was something different about Hohenheim. Hohenheim seems to know this, and expresses thanks Pinako for treating him "normally."

Pinako is old and wise, and certainly knows a thing or two about the secrets of the world and of alchemy.

See Glossary
Pinako
Hohenheim
Elric Brothers

See questions
45

47 Why did Roy Mustang join the military?

See Glossary
Roy Mustang
Ishbal Rebellion
State Alchemist

See questions
13 **48**

Having experienced the Ishbalan war, Roy Mustang wants to create a better world for the next generation. Therefore he aspires to become Fuhrer in order to change his country's political system. So why did he join the military, which caused him to become involved in the Ishbal Rebellion to begin with?

His motivation is not directly discussed, but it seems that he has been skilled at alchemy since his youth. It is possible he joined the State Alchemists in search of glory. He became known as the "Hero of Ishbal" because he saved many of his comrades. He also learned to control his fire techniques better. Even as a soldier, he places priority on preserving human life. (However, in the anime he does kill Winry's parents.) The "army" as he envisioned it, and the "real army" turned out to be two different things.

48 Is Roy's fire alchemy useless if it's raining?

In Roy's techniques, he uses the target as combustible material, and enriches the oxygen content of the surrounding air using alchemy. The spark for igniting it is created by his gloves, which are made of a material called pyrotex that produces sparks from friction. To enrich the oxygen content he uses transmutation circles in his gloves. (These are written in his own blood.) Therefore the one thing he needs is fire (he cannot make this with alchemy), but if it's raining and his gloves get wet they will no longer produce sparks.. However, as long as he has his transmutation circles, the fire source can be anything (a lighter, etc) and his fire techniques will work even in the rain. Also, although it would seem that his techniques would be affected by rain, he can use alchemy to split apart the water molecules, concentrate the hydrogen, then produce a hydrogen explosion. Roy's alchemy works on both sunny and rainy days.

See Glossary

Roy Mustang
Alchemy
Transmutation circles

See questions
47 49

49 Is it true that Roy is a womanizer?

Whether working or not, Roy often uses military phone lines to call girls. He also encrypts his alchemy notes using a girls name. Those around him call him a "ladies' man." In fact, when he's on the phone he's usually talking to Hawkeye and giving her orders (the story takes place before the advent of cellular phones). His womanizing image is sort of a cover. His use of girl's names to encrypt his alchemy notes was also part of the act.

Of course, he probably does like women, but he's not so foolish as to call them while working or otherwise mix work with his personal life.

See Glossary
Roy Mustang
Riza Hawkeye
Alchemy notes

See questions
47 48

50 Who is this person Riza Hawkeye says she wants to protect?

When Winry asks Riza why she joined the military, she replies that there is someone she wants to protect. While she doesn't say specifically who this is, it is probably Roy Mustang. Their relationship is more than just professional; Roy was the pupil of Riza's father, who is an alchemist. With the death of her father, Riza's relationship with Roy is ended for awhile, but they meet again in the Ishbalan war. In other words, they were acquainted even before entering the military.

The way she struggles to keep her calm when Riza hears Roy has been killed shows that she thinks of him as more than just her superior officer. Since she cannot show her feelings directly, she tries to protect Roy; this is her way of expressing her love for him. Another interesting fact is that Grumman is her grandfather on her mother's side.

See Glossary
Winry
Riza Hawkeye
Roy Mustang
Grumman

See questions
49

51 What does Alex Louis Armstrong think of Roy?

Despite his appearance, Armstrong is sentimental and kind. Although his family has a tradition of turning out military leaders, he is humble about his own position. In addition to alchemy, he is talented in an unusually wide range of skills, including art and tracking (all of which are family traditions). He became a State Alchemist to protect the weak, but is so disturbed by the indiscriminate attacks against women and children waged during the Ishbalan conflict, he returns to Central temporarily unable to fight any more. From then on he holds doubts about the military's policies. In fact, when he and Roy chat they seem to be probing each other and don't seem to have a very trusting relationship. However, Armstrong seems to be a good judge of people. When Armstrong learns the truth about Bradley's true identity and the corruption of the military from Roy, he believes him. He decides to stay and confront the problems, not wanting to flee again like he did at Ishbal. After this, he supports Roy by relaying messages from Roy to Edward. Although they never have a heart-to-heart talk, they trust each other implicitly.

E dward learned that the military was participating in research on the Philosopher's Stone by decoding the notes left by Marcoh. The others who initially learned of this were Maria Ross and Denny Brosh. Given that making a Philosopher's Stone requires many human lives, the participation of the military in this research is quite scandalous. Mäes Hughes also learns this, but is killed by Bradley to keep him quiet.

Bradley is the primary instigator of research on the Philosopher's Stone. If Bradley had been that worried about people finding out about this, one would expect him to try to silence Brosh, Ross and Armstrong too. But only Hughes is killed. Hughes was looking at the geographic relationships between the Lior riots and Ishbalan war, and had figured out the military's plan. This is perhaps unexpected, because Hughes does not seem like a very threatening character.

He dotes on his family, and brags about them, particularly his daughter, to anyone, anywhere, sometimes to the point where it gets annoying. However, like his friend Roy Mustang, his antics are an act to get people to drop their guard around him. He actually has a very keen mind. Of all the people who knew of the secret military research only he was killed. This must have been because only he had accurately pieced together the military's true intentions.

See Glossary

Mäes Hughes
Philosopher's Stone
Maria Ross
Denny Brosh
Roy Mustang
King Bradley

53 How deeply was Tim Marcoh involved in the creation of the Philosopher's Stone?

See Glossary
Dr. Marcoh
State Alchemist
Philosopher's Stone

Tim Marcoh is a former State Alchemist formally titled the Crystal Alchemist. This title is a reference to the Philosopher's Stones, so Marcoh probably already had in-depth knowledge of the stones when he entered the military. However, he's appalled that the material for the stones is living humans and that the finished prototypes are used by death squads in Ishbala, so he steals his data and prototypes and flees.

Taking on the alias Mauro, he hides in the countryside posing as a physician. Marcoh was probably not the person who discovered that the primary ingredient in Philosopher's Stones was living humans. However, it is certain that his prototype stone was used in the Ishbalan War. In the anime, Scar uses alchemy to transmute Philosopher's Stones, and this is probably similar to how Marcoh does it.

54 What is the technique Scar uses to destroy things?

S car is an Ishbalan and therefore a believer in the god Ishbala. His faith rejects alchemy, and Scar is fundamentally hostile towards alchemists. For this reason he disapproved of his brother, who was researching alchemy. He begins killing State Alchemists one after another out of his anger over the Ishbalan genocide, during which his brother and countrymen were killed. The destructive technique he uses to do this is actually alchemy. He performs just the decomposition step in the alchemic process, which produces a terrifying, destructive force.

During the Ishbalan genocide, Kimblee attacks Scar, but his brother saves him by acting as a human shield. Scar is not killed, but loses his right arm. His mortally wounded brother saves him by giving Scar his own right arm. So ironically Scar ends up with the right arm of an alchemist. It is this arm that allows him to perform the decomposition step of alchemy. (In the anime, he manages to perform the transmutation step too, sacrificing himself and 7000 Amestris soldiers to turn Alphonse's armor into a Philosopher's Stone using a transmutation circle drawn around the city of Lior.) The fact that Scar uses alchemy to destroy the alchemists he so hates is symbolic of the inner turmoil he feels.

See Glossary

Scar
Ishbala
Alchemy
State Alchemist
Kimblee
Philosopher's Stone
Lior

radley was born to be the Fuhrer, having been created as part of an experiment (his parents are unknown). He was the first human to be implanted with a Philosopher's Stone, creating the Homunculus Wrath. Unlike the other Homunculi, he is not an artificial being. His numerous exploits on the battlefield allow him to gain the title of Fuhrer at the young age of 44. He created the State Alchemist system shortly after to concentrate political power with the Central government, and through military intervention in other countries and suppression of domestic uprisings, cemented the military's involvement in politics.

This rise of militarism is part of the plan laid out by the Homunculi's creator, and Bradley himself is just a pawn in the game. Like the other Homunculi, Bradley is proud of the fact that he is a Homunculus and disdains humans. However, he often talks about his views on humans and religion, revealing some aspects that differ from the other Homunculi. He does not totally dismiss humans, and seems to enjoy Edward and Mustang's defiance of him, though it is unclear why. Perhaps it is because he was originally human himself, or maybe he just dislikes senseless killing. In his own way, Bradley seems to hold some sense of respect for Edward and Mustang.

In the anime, Bradley's true identity is Pride. The anime portrays him as more of a pragmatist and cold-hearted villain.

See Glossary

King Bradley
Philosopher's Stone
Homunculus
Wrath
State Alchemist
Edward
Pride

See questions
65 67

56 Why does Barry the Chopper (Number 66) join the military?

See Glossary
Barry the Chopper
Homunculi
Laboratory 5
Roy Mustang
Kimblee

Barry the Chopper is an assassin originally created by the Homunculi to guard Laboratory 5. He was originally a butcher turned serial killer who killed 23 people in Central. He is a complete psychopath, who chops up people simply because he finds it pleasant. He was scheduled to be executed, but instead had his soul sealed inside a suit of armor and made a guard at Laboratory 5.

He joins Mustang simply to gain his freedom, having not reformed his sociopathic personality in the least. However, he does seem to have learned some restraint. He behaves calmly in the detention center, and he refrains from killing when ordered to do so. He is sort of the counterpart to Kimblee, the psychopathic bomber who joins with the Homunculi.

L ing Yao is the Xing Emperor's twelfth son. His clan, the Yao clan, consists of 500,000 people. It can be said that their fate depends on whether or not Ling is selected to be the next Xing Emperor. Ling seems friendly and light-hearted, but he's very cool and collected. His burning desire to learn the secrets of immortality ultimately stems from his loyalty to his clan. He cares for his people, and therefore feels deep anger at Bradley (Wrath) who thinks nothing of his citizens' lives.

On the other hand, Ling is a pragmatist and not too fussy about how he obtains his goals. From childhood, he has been taught that making it to the top requires great strength. Just as Bradley became Fuhrer by becoming a Homunculus, and Roy Mustang will use virtually any means to change his country, Ling Yao is committed to becoming the emperor no matter the cost. He also feels he must justify the sacrifices of people like

Ran Fan, who gives up an arm to help him; he accepts the Philosopher's Stone in order to become immortal. As a result, Ling's soul now inhabits the same body as the Homunculus Greed, although Ling is struggling to regain complete control.

58 Who is the character known as "Father"?

Father is a mysterious character who lives deep under Central City's military base and produces Homunculi from his own body.

What kind of person is he? Outwardly, he resembles Hohenheim, the father of the Elric brothers. Like Hohenheim, who never seems to age and can survive apparently any attack, Father has lived for hundreds of years, and has a third eye from which he can produce Philosopher's Stones;he's not your average guy. He can also perform alchemy without moving his body (or even making a transmutation circle), and can prevent alchemy from being performed in a fairly wide radius around himself.

Although his identity has yet to be revealed, it is possible that he's the "legendary philosopher" who brought alchemy to Amestris from Xerxes hundreds of years ago.

See Glossary

Father
Central City
Homunculi
Erlic Brothers
Hohenheim
Philosopher's Stone
Xerxes

See questions
59 **60**

Dante is a character who only appears in the anime. She plays a role similar to that of Father in the manga. Dante was Izumi Curtis's instructor. Once an old woman who lived a secretive life in the forest, she is able to take over other people's bodies with the power of the Philosopher's Stone, prolonging her life indefinitely. She is a very high level alchemist, performing feats such as transmutation without a transmutation circle, and using a baby to open the Gate of Truth. Throughout the course of the series, her cruel, self-serving nature emerges, and she takes over the body of her pupil Lyra. In stark contrast to Izumi, Dante is a misanthrope. This is why she lives like a hermit in the woods.

In contrast to Father, who appears to be using the Homunculi to affect some sort of cataclysmic change in the world, Dante uses them to further her selfish goal of living forever by continually seizing control of other people's bodies.

She both tries to keep the secrets of the Philosopher's Stones hidden, while leaking certain information to further her ends. She plans to create demand for a complete stone by inciting war, leading someone to create one, which she will then steal. To this end she uses the Homunculi as her agents. She keeps them in her service by promising to use the Philosopher's Stone to make them real humans. She only really trusts Envy and Bradley (Pride), and has no faith in Wrath, whose arm and leg she takes to punish him for trying to use the Philosopher's Stone on his own.

Her ultimate motivation is immortality, and this is why she also steals Lyra's body. Up until now, Dante has been unable to reconcile her soul with her host bodies, causing the body to rot while still alive. This process starts to accelerate, causing her to begin studying the Gate (this also means she needs the Philosopher's Stone more quickly than planned).

At the end of the series, she attempts to use Al and Rose as human sacrifices to send

See Glossary

Hohenheim through the Gate and counter Edward. In the end, she is unexpectedly devoured by Gluttony, in a sense reaping what she has sown (although her death is left a little ambiguous).

See questions

58 60

part 04

Homunculus' Secrets

The Homunculi are living beings and seem to have been named after the seven deadly sins from the Purgatorio portion of Dante's Divine Comedy--Pride, Envy, Wrath, Sloth, Greed, Gluttony and Lust. Each has the seal of Ouroboros tattooed somewhere on their body. However, the methods of and reasons for creating the Homunculi are completely different in the manga and anime.

Manga

In the manga Homunculi are created by a character known as "Father" who lives deep underneath a military complex. They are created from philosopher's stones. Father names each of the philosopher's stones after the seven sins, and the Homunculi created from them take on some of the characteristics of that sin (for example, Greed is avaricious, and so on). Although they basically work for Father, some, like Greed, break away and sign on to other causes.

Some of the Homunculi, like Gluttony, are born from Father's chest area, while others, like Wrath and the second incarnation of Greed, are produced by impregnating a human body with a Philosopher's Stone. As the manga series is not complete yet, Father's reasons for creating the Homunculi are unclear as of this writing. Also, it is as yet unclear whether the Philosopher's Stones used by Father to create the Homunculi are the same as the Philosopher's Stones produced by Marcoh and used during the Ishbal Rebellion.

Anime

In the anime, Homunculi are created during failed attempts at human transmutation, and at first do not have human form. By feeding on incomplete Philosopher's Stones, called Red Stones (anime only), they can take on human form. Consequently, each Homunculus has a weakness: the remains (relics) of the human they were created from. (In the case of Wrath, there are no relics as Izumi sent the transmuted child to the other side of the Gate.) The Homunculi are not exactly like the humans that proceeded them; Lust and Sloth in particular have very different personalities. As a result, the Homunculi are continually tormented by the memories of the humans they're based on. It seems that the use of the seven deadly sins as names by the character Dante was somewhat arbitrary, and for the most part, the names don't have much to do with the Homunculi themselves. Compared with the manga, almost all the anime Homunculi have more ruthless personalities.

They are essentially motivated by their desire to become human (with the exception of Envy and Greed). Dante uses their feelings to further his goal of acquiring Philosopher's Stones. Not all the Homunculi were create by Dante. In more than a few cases, Homunculi created by other people were given Red Stones and brought into the group. Lust, Sloth and Wrath are the representative examples of this.

To summarize, in the manga, Homunculi are created by Father for some as yet unknown purpose. In contrast, in the anime,

Homunculi are the result of humans attempting the "sin" of human transmutation. They are not necessarily created for a specific purpose.

See Glossary

Homunculi
Dante
Pride
Envy
Wrath
Sloth
Greed
Gluttony
Lust
Ouroboros
Father
Philosopher's Stone
Dr. Marcoh
Ishbal Rebellion
Human transmutation
Red Stones
Izumi Curtis

See questions
16

61 Lust's Secrets

L ust is one of the first Homunculi introduced in both the manga and anime. Her appearance is that of a beautiful woman, with an Ouroboros insignia on her chest. She can extend her fingernails, which become sharp blades, which she can fully control. The power of those weapons has earned her the name "Ultimate Lance."

In the manga she was the second Homunculus created. She is created to be the Father's right arm in coordinating and carrying out his plans. As such, she is active both on and offstage, performing tasks such as trailing the Elrics, and becoming intimate with Jean Havoc in order to get information on Mustang's group.

She battles Mustang at the Third Laboratory. Although she seems to have the upper hand at first, his deep resolve eventually defeats her. She leaves behind some strange last words on dying. It is unclear whether there will be a second incarnation of

Lust (her Philosopher's Stone was destroyed, so this seems impossible).

In the anime, she was based on Scar's brother's dead lover. She was created when the man tried to perform a human transmutation on his lover. Lust seeks out people who have the ability to perform transmutation, and persuades them to seek Philosopher's Stones in order to resurrect loved ones or to save their hometowns from the ravages of war (the war and other tragedies are intentionally set up by Dante to serve his ends). Although Lust is ruthless, she is the most human of the Homunculi and strongly hopes to use the Philosopher's Stones to become human. She has something approaching a friendship with Sloth, perhaps because they are in similar situations. Toward the end of her life, she regains some of her original memories, and can no longer bear being Dante's slave. She breaks with Dante to join the Elrics. She helps set up a seal to trap Sloth, but ends up sealed and killed by a furious Wrath. To her, death seems to be a release from suffering, and she breaths her last peacefully. It seems there was another incarnation of Lust before her, but the details are unknown.

62 Gluttony's Secrets

Gluttony is onethe first Homunculi introduced in both the manga and anime. His Ouroboros insignia is on his tongue.

He looks like a child with a round face and body (the model for his character was apparently a snowman). He has the ability to eat literally anything, which he uses along with his near invulnerability and giant body to perform charging attacks.

His personality is that of an easygoing, innocent child. For this reason, he is conspicuously passive, waiting for permission from his comrades before attacking and showing little initiative of his own. He is particularly attached to Lust, becoming very depressed in both the manga and anime when she's killed.

In contrast to the other Homunculi, Gluttony was created with a specific purpose in mind, both in the manga and anime. Japanese fans speculate that this his aforementioned lack of will is related to this.

In the Manga he was the sixth Homunculus created. Gluttony was born from the Father's failed attempt at recreating the Gate of Truth, producing a "False Gate of Truth" instead. As a result, Gluttony's body houses an abnormal void that allows him to consume things larger than himself. Anything Gluttony eats is sent to this void area. When angry, his voice changes and his stomach splits open, like a giant vertical mouth, revealing tusk-like ribs. In the middle of this there is an eye, which makes it resemble the Gate of Truth. With this mouth he can swallow anything within reach (however, he does not necessarily have to be angry to do this, as shown when Envy gives him permission to swallow Ling during their battle.) The Homunculi are not immortal, and can only regenerate a certain number of times. In the manga, Gluttony was weakened to the point of death, and is basically dead for the moment, although Father still has his Philosopher's Stone.

In the anime, it is unclear who his human base is. According to Dante, Gluttony was created to produce Philosopher's Stones and Red Stones. Gluttony often worked with

Lust, and was severely depressed when she died. When Gluttony stops following orders Dante, who wants him to eat Alphonse's Philosopher's Stone and change it into a pure stone, turns him into a mindless being ruled by hunger. In the final episode, Gluttony and Dante disappear in the elevator, and it appears that Gluttony has devoured Dante (while this is not explicitly stated, it is assumed to be what happened, and the reemergence of Gluttony in Fullmetal Alchemist the Movie: Conqueror of Shamballa seems to confirm it).

See Glossary

Gluttony
Homunculi
Ouroboros
Lust
Father
Gate
Philosopher's Stone
Alphonse
Fullmetal Alchemist

63 Envy's Secrets

Envy's Ouroboros insignia is on his left thigh.

In the Manga he was the fourth Homunculus created by Father. His true form is utterly inhuman -like a giant, eight-legged lizard. His right eye is normal, but his left eye is composed of eight small eyes. He can change his appearance at will, turning into various people, dogs, horses, or whatever takes his fancy. He normally assumes the form of a long-haired, androgynous youth. He can also transform parts of his body into weapons during battles. Furthermore, unlike the other Homunculi, not only is his Philosopher's Stone composed of the concentrated souls of the citizens of Xerxes, but these souls also live on within him. He has a complex over his hideous true form, and becomes angry whenever anyone calls him "ugly" or "monstrous." Once he reverts to his true form, he cannot take on other forms for some time.

As is evident by his actions during the murder of Hughes and the way he jeers Edward and Dr. Marcoh, he disdains human emotions, and has a sarcastic, dry wit. He is probably the most brutal and outright bloodthirsty of the Homunculi. In both the manga and anime, his actions toward humans can only be described as diabolical, but his motivations are a bit different. In the manga, disguised as a member of the moderate faction, he fires the shot that begins the Ishbarlan war and, disguised as Cornello, starts the insurgency of Lior. This and his other actions are always performed in obedience to Father.

He sometimes mouths off to Lust, but on learning she has been defeated, he becomes distressed, indicating he considers her a friend (or maybe family). His suspicions that the false Marcoh made by Scar is a living thing also shows that he's not merely a homicidal maniac.

In the anime, Envy is created from the son of Dante and Hohenheim. Hohenheim attempts a human transmutation on his son, who died of mercury poisoning. However, Envy was discarded and lived a miserable life, leading him to become even more evil than in the manga. In his original form he closely resembled Hohenheim (or, in his younger days, Edward). The major difference between Envy and the other Homunculi is that Envy understands Dante's objectives (since she is the mother of the person he's based on) and wants to make humans suffer, rather than become human. For this reason, when he is with his partners he puts on an act of friendship. He is also strongly resentful of his father, who is also the Elrics' father, and toward the end his terrible nature emerges and he "kills" Edward. Afterward, he rushes to the other side of the Gate to meet Hohenheim, but in his dragon (Leviathan) form. His last words before disappearing (translated literally) are: "When the human race is extinct, at last I will be able to forget. Forget why I was born..."

S ee Glossary

Envy
Ouroboros
Father
Philosopher's Stone
Xerxes
Mäes Hughes
Dr. Marcoh
Cornello
Lior
Scar
Dante
Hohenheim

64 *Greed's Secrets*

Greed's Ouroboros insignia is on the back of his left hand.

He can freely alter the strength of the bonds of the carbon in his body, turning his skin into a diamond-hard substance. This ability has earned him the title of "Ultimate Shield." This shield can be used for offense as well as defense. While Greed can cover his entire body with this substance, he prefers not to because it looks somewhat unaesthetic. It's somewhat unclear which is his true form--his normal appearance or shield form.

He was the third Homunculus to be created. His catch-phrase is "There's no such thing as no such thing."

In the manga, it has been 100 years since he left Father, in whose service he felt dissatisfied. After this, he gathers around him a band of misfits and founds the Devil's Nest, where he lives in luxury. However, the Nest is wiped out during Bradley's campaign.

After his defeat by Bradley, Greed is taken back to Father. Father asks Greed to again join with him, but Greed refuses on the grounds that his own desires will never be satisfied working for Father. As a result, Father extracts and reappropriates Greed's Philosopher's Stone. Greed is absent for awhile after this, but later his Philosopher's Stone is implanted in Ling. He is then recreated as a human-based Homunculus, similar to Wrath.

While the second Greed has the same soul as the first, he retains no memories of his predecessor and is still loyal to Father. Also, Ling's consciousness still remains inside him. Greed is somewhat sympathetic to the residual personality of Ling, sometimes listening to Ling's requests; the two seem to get along and have a sort of emerging friendship.

In the anime, Greed is based on someone Dante once loved (the details are sketchy). He was created by Dante during an experiment. Dante tries to control him emotionally, but cannot and ends up sealing him. Greed breaks out after 140 years, and gathers his army of chimera underlings. In the end, he is trapped and loses his stone, after which he is killed by Edward who has been led to believe that Dante is dead. With his dying breath, he reveals the secret of the Homunculi's weakness to Edward.

See Glossary

Greed
Ouroboros
Ultimate Shield
Homunculus
Devil's Nest
King Bradley
Philosopher's Stone
Ling Yao
Wrath
Father
Dante

65 Wrath's Secrets

Wrath's appearance is completely different in the manga and anime.

In the manga he was the seventh Homunculus created. He is actually King Bradley. His Ouroboros insignia is on his left eye.

Unlike the other Homunculi, he is a human that was changed into a Homunculus by being implanted with a Philosopher's Stone and surviving its usually lethal energy. According to the other Homunculi, he was created as a sort of ultimate trump card. As he was the youngest, until the second incarnation of Greed came along, the others, particularly Envy, looked down on Wrath.

His Homunculus ability is his "Ultimate Eye," which is keen enough to see the trajectory of a bullet. He uses his physical prowess together with amazing vision to defeat enemies using a sword. His defeat of Greed in the blink of an eye indicates that his abilities are high even compared with other Homunculi.

In his human guise, he is able to perform roles the other Homunculi cannot, such as recruiting State Alchemists in order to find talented alchemists.

On the other hand, in the anime, he's portrayed as a child. His Ouroboros insignia is on the sole of his right foot. He is based on Izumi's child. After being born from a human transmutation, he was sent to the other side of the Gate where he grew up. He has the ability to freely combine himself with other matter. This ability allowed him to fuse with Edward's arm and leg, giving him enough of a human form to escape from the Gate. Originally, he is an innocent child, but his personality turns vicious after being given a Red Stone by Envy. Normally, Homunculi cannot use alchemy, but wrath is able to perform unique alchemic techniques since he possesses Ed's arm and leg. This combined with his ability to fuse with matter make him a powerful adversary. Furthermore, he lacks vulnerability to his predecessor's remains, since Izumi sent the relics of the child he's based on into the Gate. He is however terrified of the sound of crying babies. Starved of motherly affection, he gloms onto Sloth as his surrogate "mama." When Sloth is sealed by Edward, Wrath entreats Dante to bring her back using her Philosopher's Stone. This only enrages Dante, who opens the Gate, causing Wrath to lose Edward's limbs, rendering Wrath incapable of performing alchemy. Wrath also is responsible for sealing Lust, calling her a traitor for her part in trapping Sloth. Because his human form was dependent on receiving Red Stones and Edward's arm and leg, without them he never recovers. In the end, Winry gives Wrath some automail, originally meant for Edward, to replace Wrath's lost limbs.

Ⓢee Glossary

Wrath
Homunculus
King Bradley
Ouroboros
Izumi Curtis
Human transmutation
Gate
Red Stone
Winry

66 Sloth's Secrets

L ike Wrath, Sloth's appearance is completely different in the manga and anime.

In the manga he was the fifth Homunculus created (in the anime Sloth is the seventh, created in 1910). His Ouroboros insignia is on his left shoulder.

In the manga he appears to be huge and muscular, although as of yet he's only appeared in two panels so it's difficult to tell. He has been digging some sort of hole or tunnel for 100 years, but as his name suggests he frequently slacks off, and as a result hasn't finished whatever his task is.

In the anime, Sloth is a different character. Her Ouroboros insignia is on her left breast. She is based on Trisha, the Elrics' mother. Her alias is Colonel Juliet Douglas, private secretary to King Bradley. Unlike Trisha, her optimistic predecessor, Sloth is cold and never expresses emotion. However, like Lust, she strongly wants to become human and to this end follows Dante's commands loyally. She has the ability to turn her body into liquid. This lets her enter virtually any place, and enables her to ensnare enemies or pulverize them with a waterspout during battles. It is futile to attack her directly. Her personality is a combination of Trisha's and her own. Since she possesses some of Trisha's memories, she is aware that she has died. As a result she suffers from two personalities-- that of the Homunculus Sloth and already deceased Trisha. Her desire to kill Edward and his brother is her attempt to reject the Trisha part of her. She fights Edward trying to capture Alphonse, who has become a Philosopher's Stone. The battle goes her way until Wrath, who has earlier absorbed Trisha's remains, merges with and paralyzes Sloth. Edward changes her body into the volatile substance ethanol. As she evaporates she utters some last words, which could be taken to mean that she has fully regained her identity as Trisha. Or, they may have been Trisha's words but spoken through Sloth--it's left unclear.

See Glossary

Sloth
Wrath
Ouroboros
Trisha
Colonel Juliet Douglas
King Bradley
Lust
Dante
Edward
Alphonse
Philosopher's Stone

67 Pride's Secrets

The thing named Pride is an artificial being. His appearance is completely different in the manga and anime. In the manga, he was the first Homunculus created. He first appears only as a voice.

Although he has not yet been shown, he is distinguished in the manga by the rather polite language he uses (at least in the Japanese version). His ability to silence Envy seems to indicate he is in a leadership position among the Homunculi.

At one point, Wrath (King Bradley) casually mentions he enjoyed having his plans disrupted, but Pride keeps this secret from Father. It has been speculated that he and Wrath are in charge of selecting alchemists to become State Alchemists.

In the anime, Pride is actually King Bradley. It is unclear who his human base is. He is Dante's greatest work and her loyal subject. He conducts the armed forces in order to efficiently collects human lives to obtain Philosopher's Stones. While keeping the armed forces distanced from the Philosopher's Stones, he is said to play a large role among the Homunculi in starting wars and internal conflicts. Pride entrusts his weakness (the skull of the man he was created from) to his adopted son Selim. Unaware of its true importance, Selim ends up bringing it to Roy Mustang during a battle. Furious, Pride strangles his son, but it's too late; Mustang traps him and burns Pride until he uses up all his life. In the manga and anime, the mechanisms for aging are different. In the anime, Pride seems to able to alter his appearance, and changes to give the impression of aging.

See Glossary

Pride
Homunculus
Envy
Wrath
Dante
Philosopher's Stone
Selim
Roy Muntang
King Bradley

68 What was the purpose of creating the Homunculi?

In the anime, Homunculi are created accidentally during failed attempts at the forbidden practice of human transmutation, and given life with Red Stones. They are not created for any particular purpose. They would not exist in the first place if no one attempted human transmutation. In other words, in the anime the Homunculi are the price paid for committing a "sin" (attempting to create human life in defiance of nature). Normally they would not work toward any purpose at all. Although Dante uses them to collect stones for her own personal ends, this is not necessarily the personal purpose of the Homunculi themselves.

In the manga, the Homunculi are created by Father for a specific purpose. All the Homunculi are created from a Philosopher's Stone, and they are incapable of disobeying Father (with the exception of Greed). They all work towards achieving Father's plans.

Furthermore, since they are all based on deep-rooted sins (Envy, Greed, etc.) in Father's soul, their personalities are quite different.

In the anime, the Homunculi's personalities are based on the people they were transmuted from.

See Glossary

Homunculi
Human transmutation
Red Stones
Dante
Greed
Father
Envy
Philosopher's Stone

69 Why does Father create the Homunculi?

See Glossary
Father
Homunculi
Elric brothers
Hohenheim
Xerxes

The manga series is still a work in progress, and Father's intentions have not been made clear yet, but it seems he has drastic plans in store that will affect the entire human race. Since Father bears a striking resemblance to the Elric brothers' father Hohenheim (who never seems to age and is apparently immortal and impervious to bullets), it is probable that like Hohenheim, Father too is not a normal human. Given his extraordinary alchemy skills, he might be the legendary philosopher who started the spread of alchemy from Xerxes. Furthermore, given that the Homunculi he creates are based on the Seven Deadly Sins, he may be attempting to exact some sort of justice from the human race.

70 Why do the Homunculi have special powers?

I n the manga, Homunculi are created from the Philosopher's Stones produced by Father. These in turn are composed of human souls and contain vast amounts of energy. This energy gives the Homunculi powers beyond those of normal humans, allowing them to turn their bodies into weapons. Although they cannot perform alchemy, this only means that they cannot transmute substances beyond their own bodies; they are capable of turning their own flesh into other forms. This too is probably due to the fact that the core of each Homunculus is a Philosopher's Stone. The Philosopher's Stone gives them the power to overcome the Law of Equivalent Exchange. Thus, they can transmute portions of their own bodies to give them special abilities.

In the anime, the Homunculi gain their special abilities from the fact that they are by-products of human transmutation, and from the power of the Red Stones.

See Glossary

Homunculi
Philosopher's Stone
Father
Alchemy
Red Stones

71 Do the Homunculi have any weaknesses?

The Homunculi are virtually immortal, and can regenerate even after being killed. However, in the anime they have one clear weakness. They are vulnerable to the remains and relics of the person they were transmuted from. If a Homunculus touches such an object, it is paralyzed. It seems that some sort of reaction occurs between the object and the Homunculus's body.

In the manga, the Homunculi do not have this sort of clear weakness, but if the Philosopher's Stones in their bodies are removed, they die. Also, as in the case of Gluttony, if a Homunculus dies repeatedly it becomes incapable of regenerating. Its Philosopher's Stone has to be removed and returned to Father's body. So it seems they are not actually immortal, but can only regenerate a certain number of times. Also, as seen when Ling becomes the new Greed (by being injected with Greed's Philosopher's Stone), it seems that the upward limit on Homunculus in the manga is in fact seven, corresponding with the Father's seven sins.

In the anime, the Homunculi are created through human transmutation, so logically there is no limit on how many can be created.

See Glossary

Homunculi
Philosopher's Stone
Gluttony
Ling Yao
Greed

A

Alexander

The Tucker's family dog. It's a huge animal that charges Ed whenever he visits. Shou Tucker, under pressure of his evaluation, turns Alexander and Nina into chimera. After that, his fate is the same as Nina's.

In the anime, Alexander lives in Central with Shou Tucker.

Alex Louis Armstrong

A Major in the military. A State Alchemist also known as the Strong Arm Alchemist. Despite his appearance, he is sentimental and kind. Although his family has a tradition of turning out military leaders, he is humble about his own position. In addition to alchemy, he is talented in an unusually wide range of skills, including art and tracking (all of which are family traditions). He has two sisters. Olivier is a military woman like him, but so beautiful it's hard to believe they're related. Catherine is quiet, but strong enough to lift a piano.

He became a State Alchemist to protect the weak, but is so disturbed by the indiscriminate attacks against women and children waged during the Ishbal conflict, he returns to Central temporarily unable to fight any more. From then on he holds doubts about the military's policies.

Armstrong learns the truth about Bradley's true identity and the corruption of the military from Roy. He considers quitting the military altogether, but decides to stay and confront the problems, not wanting to flee again like he did at Ishbal.

Alphonse Elric

The other hero of the story. Ed's younger brother. Often goes by Al.

When he's about 9, his mother dies from an illness, so he and his brother Edward study alchemy under Izumi with the goal of bringing back their mother through human transmutation. Eventually, they return home and attempt unsuccessfully to perform the transmutation, during which his brother Ed binds his soul to a suit of armor. He travels with his brother, as they are both working toward the same goals.

He has a very warm, kind personality. He cares deeply about his brother, and

understands him better than anyone else. He's remarkably mature for his age, perhaps from having to keep an eye on his emotional older brother.

During battles, he uses simple physical attacks, taking advantage of his large, armored body and his innate speed. In the manga, her acquires the ability to perform alchemy without a transmutation circle. It's revealed that he's never lost a fight with Ed, so he must be pretty strong even before he gets the armor.

In the anime, he fights Kimblee with Scar in Lior. Scar beats Kimblee, but on the verge of death Kimblee transforms Al's body into an explosive substance. To save Al, Scar uses the souls of 7000 soldiers to create a Philosopher's Stone and transmutes Al's armor body itself into a Philosopher's Stone. After this, he and Ed flee from the Homunculi, who are seeking Philosopher's Stones, and are taken to Dante's underground city after falling into Tucker's trap. There, Al resurrects Ed with a successful human transmutation, using the Philosopher's Stone that comprises his body. Ed then resurrects Al, who revives as his 10 year-old self with no memory of events since the attempt to revive their mother. He goes to study under Izumi, believing he will someday be reunited with Ed.

B

Bald

Member of an extremist group (called the Aono Dan or "Blue Team" in the Japanese). He attempts to hijack a train and take Hakuro and his family hostage in order to free his imprisoned leader. He has a low-grade automail left arm (which contains a hidden knife). He's defeated on the train by the Elric brothers. On arriving at the station, he gets loose again, but is stopped by Mustang.

Barry the Chopper (Number 66)

An assassin who guards Laboratory 5 and a serial killer who butchered 23 people in Central. He enjoys chopping people up. He was scheduled to be executed, but was instead sealed inside a suit of armor and made a guard at Laboratory 5. While fighting Al, Barry instills doubt in him about Ed. After the battle, Barry flees to the laboratory.

He later falls in love with Hawkeye, and is protected by Mustang. Barry decides the best way to gain freedom is to destroy the Homunculi, so he allies with Mustang. However, he eventually discovers his former body, which has been implanted with the soul of a chimera. Trying to kill his old

body, he meets Lust and in the ensuing battle his Blood Seal becomes exposed and is destroyed by his own flesh body.

In the anime, he appears before being arrested. Three years previously he had killed his wife and become a serial killer. In the end he is brought down by the concerted alchemy of Ed, Al and Scar.

Basque Grand

A colonel in the military (later promoted to brigadier general). Also called the Iron Blood Alchemist. Originally, he administered Laboratory 5.

Probably the character with the most differences in his manga and anime incarnations. The only common point is that he was supposedly killed by Scar.

A war veteran. His nickname seems to be a reference to Otto von Bismarck's "iron and blood" policy.

In the manga, he seems to be an honorable soldier. During the Ishbal war, although a colonel, he is at the front lines trying to keep his men from dying. He also kills his own brigadier general after the latter orders him to exterminate a group of surrendering Ishbalans, and allows their leader to meet with King Bradley. However, as nominal administrator of Laboratory 5, he will be the scapegoat if the experiments conducted there are discovered.

In the anime, he is in charge of the military's most secret projects, such as the chimera and Philosopher's Stones. He is also one of the primary users of alchemy for warfare. He also brings total war to Ishbal by deploying a Philosopher's Stone. Furthermore, he forces Mustang to kill the Rockbells for impeding the military. Grand's character is almost the exact opposite in the manga and anime. In the anime, he is killed by Scar, shortly after obtaining Marcoh's Philosopher's Stone.

Belsio

Friend of Nash. Only appears in the anime. Unmarried and works on a farm. Worried about Elisa's illness.

Bido

One of Greed's subordinates. He's a lizard/human chimera. His lizard abilities allow him to climb up vertical surfaces. He's given the assignment of provoking the Elric brothers. He survives the raid on the Devil's Nest in the manga.

In the anime, he's killed during the raid.

Black Hayate

Hawkeye's dog. In the Japanese series, the dog is nicknamed "Buraha" (a contraction of his full name). Black Hayate was

abandoned as a puppy, and adopted by Fuery before eventually ending up under Riza Hawkeye's care. Perhaps a result of Riza's rather severe disciplinary measures, Black Hayate becomes a brave dog, helping his master by attacking Gluttony.

Buccaneer

A Captain in the military. Olivier's subordinate. Buccaneer has a distinctive catfish beard. He is equipped with automail specialized for cold environments. He teases Ed over his automail.

C

Catherine Elle Armstrong

Armstrong's little sister. She looks nothing like her brother, being beautiful and stylish. However, her hobbies include lifting pianos over her head. She and Havoc are set up on a blind date, but she rejects his advances--it seems she prefers muscular guys like her older brother.

Clara

A nurse from the city Aquroya, a city that floats in a lake, somewhat similar to Venice. An alchemist. Only appears in the anime. Clara is the real name of the thief Psiren. A kindly nurse by day, at night she becomes the alchemist thief Psiren. She has an alchemic mark above her chest with which she can cause explosions. However, she doesn't steal for material gain, she simply wants to create some excitement in her slowly sinking city. She is briefly captured by the police while the Elric brothers are in Aquroya, but almost immediately escapes again. She is currently continuing to revitalize her city through theft.

Clause

A girl living in Linta. Only appears in the anime. She's a bit of a tomboy and very competitive. When she first meets Ed and Al, they actually mistake her for a young boy due to her clothes. She's pursuing the truth behind the mysterious death of her older sister.

Cornello

Leader of the Leto religion. He claims to be the emissary of Leto, the sun god. Uses an incomplete Philosopher's Stone to perform "miracles" and gather followers. His ultimate goal is to create his own military state. However, the Elric brothers expose him. Lust kills Cornello, since he's of no further use. In the manga, Cornello is killed by Lust and his dead body is eaten by Gluttony. In the anime, Cornello is eaten alive by Gluttony.

Cray

A missionary of the Leto faith. Assists Cornello. Attacks the Elric brothers on Cornello's orders, but gets beaten up instead. After the attack on Lior, Cray discovers that Cornello has been replaced by Envy and is eaten by Gluttony.

D

Dante

Only appears in the anime. She plays a role similar to that of Father in the manga. She was the instructor that taught Izumi. She tries to keep the secrets of the Philosopher's Stones hidden, while leaking out certain information about them. She plans to create a demand for a stone by inciting war, leading someone to create one, which she will then steal.

At the end of series, she attempts to use Al and Rose as human sacrifices to send Hohenheim through the Gate and counter Ed. In the end, she is unexpectedly devoured by Gluttony, in a sense reaping what she had sown.

Dominic LeCoulte

An automail mechanic. Very skilled, but very stubborn. Even so, he's very kind to his grandchild. Almost insists that Paninya accept his weaponized automail limbs. In his youth, he was hit by Pinako (who was riding a motorcycle). This lead him to fear Pinako, the "Leopardess of Risembool", and was perhaps related to his refusal to accept Winry as a pupil. The scar on his chin is from this incident. In the anime, he lectures Paninya on automail, telling her that it's not just mechanical. He views automail as genuine limbs.

Den

The Rockbell's family dog. Very protective of Pinako. Den's front left leg is automail. Female.

Denny Brosh

A sergeant in the military. Armstrong's subordinate. A serious but fun-loving character. He is assigned, along with Ross, to act as the Elric brothers' bodyguard. He secretly has a crush on Ross, but never gets around to telling her. In the anime, on seeing Hohenheim chatting Ross up, Brosh cries his eyes out. In the manga, when she's arrested he tries to make an alibi for her, but is turned down. His face shows what he's thinking like an open book, and for this reason he hasn't been told that Ross is still alive.

Dorchet

One of Greed's subordinates. He's a dog/human chimera. Originally a member of the military. He's optimistic and loyal. His dog half gives him a keen sense of smell and speed. His weapon is a sword. He's not exactly weak, but loses a lot since he's always faced with superior foes, such as the Elric brothers and Izumi. Killed by Bradley during the attack on Devil's Nest.

In the anime, it's revealed that he was in the Special Forces with Loa and Martel.

E

Edward Elric

The hero of the story. Often simply called Ed.

With his gold hair and eyes, he is the Fullmetal Alchemist. When he's about 10, his mother dies from an illness, so he and his brother Alphonse study alchemy under Izumi with the goal of bringing back their mother through human transmutation. Eventually, they return home and attempt unsuccessfully to perform the transmutation. Edward loses his left leg and his brother. To save his brother, Edward sacrifices his own right arm to bind Alphonse's soul to a suit of armor. Having lost part of his own body, and his brother's entire body, Edward is on the verge of despair when Mustang suggests he join the State Alchemists. He replaces his right arm and left leg with automail, and at 12 becomes the youngest person ever to acquire a State Alchemist license. In order to recover his lost limbs and his brother's body, the two set out to find the Philosopher's Stone. He is very impatient and becomes emotional easily. He is also a realist who does not believe in anything he considers unscientific. He is very caring towards the people he loves, such as Al and Winry, and becomes furious at those who try to harm them. He feels responsible for the loss of his brothers' body. On the other hand, he can't bring himself to tell Winry directly how he feels about her, a fact which shows his more boyish side.

He is a powerful alchemist, as shown by the fact that he lost part of his body, returned from the Truth, and is the youngest person ever to acquire the State Alchemists' license. Having seen the Truth, he gained the ability to perform alchemy using just his hands (i.e. with no transmutation circle needed). Compared to other alchemists, he can perform a wide range of techniques, but excels at metals.

Elisa

Lamac's daughter. Only appears in the anime. Helps Belsio with the farm work. Comes down with the mysterious disease caused by the Red Water.

Elysia Hughes

Hughes' daughter. In the manga, she recently turned three. She's a sweet and innocent child. Winry adores her like an older sister.

Envy

One of the Homunculi. His Ouroboros insignia is on his left thigh.

He can change his appearance at will, turning into various people, dogs, horses, or whatever takes his fancy. He normally assumes the form of a long-haired, androgynous youth. He can also transform parts of his body into weapons during battles, but is unable to reproduce complex objects.

Envy

One of the Homunculi. His Ouroboros insignia is on his left thigh.

He can change his appearance at will, turning into various people, dogs, horses, or whatever takes his fancy. He normally assumes the form of a long-haired, androgynous youth. He can also transform parts of his body into weapons during battles, but is unable to reproduce complex objects.

F

Father

The "parent" of the Homunculi. He lives in a castle deep beneath Central. In the Japanese dialog, the Homunculi seem to refer to him by several different Japanese words that all mean "father" (Chichiue, Otousama, Oyajidono, etc). His real name is unknown at this point.

With the third eye on his forehead, he can create Philosopher's Stones, create false and true Gates, and perform alchemy regardless of the power environment and law of Equivalent Exchange. He can also render powerless any Amestris alchemic technique from being used against him. He creates the Homunculi from Philosopher's Stones he produces from his own body, and gives them life by sharing his own soul with them. He draws their names from the Seven Deadly Sins.

He and Van Hohenheim seem to have some connection, and seem to know each other well.

Fletcher Tringum

Russell's little brother. Only appears in the anime. Poses as Al. As opposed to Ed, who resents his father, Fletcher respects his dad.

Focker

A captain in the military. Subordinate to Hughes and Sheska's superior. He only appears in the manga. He works at the court-martial hall.

Frank Archer

Only appears in the anime. A lieutenant colonel in the military (later promoted to colonel). Takes over Hughes' post when he's killed in the line of duty. He has a ruthless character, and never concerns himself with moral questions, traits which make him very valuable to the military. Instrumental in getting Kimblee reinstated to the military. During the Lior campaign, he gets caught in Scar's transmutation and loses half his body. He reappears after being fitted with automail to replace the missing parts. He is finally killed by Hawkeye as he attempts to eliminate Mustang.

Fu

An elderly man whose family has served Ling's household for generations. Ran Fan's grandfather. As Ran Fan's instructor he is very strict, but as her grandfather he loves her deeply. Like Ran Fan he normally wears a mask, but his is white. He has a wealth of experience, and takes pride in his excellent martial arts abilities. When Ling is arrested for illegally entering Amestris, Fu breaks him out. He also helps Ross escape from the Homunculi and takes her back to Xing. Afterward he returns to Central, but leaves again with Ran Fan.

G

Garfiel

An automail mechanic. A resident of Rush Valley, he instructs Winry. Although living an "alternative lifestyle," he is an excellent mechanic, and helps Winry reach her potential. Unlike the Spartan relationship the Elric brothers have with their mentor, Izumi, Winry and Garfiel have a more friendly relationship. Garfiel's "sexiness" (as he calls it) sometimes makes his male customers uneasy. His physique is on par with Armstrong's.

Gluttony

One of the Homunculi. His Ouroboros insignia is on his tongue.

He looks like a child with a round face and body. He has the ability to eat literally anything, which he uses along with his near invulnerability and giant body to perform charging attacks.

Gracia Hughes

Hughes' wife. An excellent cook, good wife and wise mother. She specializes in apple pie. When the Elric brothers become mixed up in her husband's problems, she advises them to press ahead.

Greed

One of the Homunculi. His Ouroboros insignia is on the back of his left hand. He can freely alter the strength of the bonds of the carbon in his body, turning his skin into a diamond-hard substance. This ability has earned him the title of "Ultimate Shield." This shield can be used for offense as well as defense.

Grumman

A lieutenant general in the military. Commander of the Eastern Headquarters. Hawkeye's grandfather and Mustang's superior. Appears to be an affable old man, but given that he's beaten Mustang at chess 97 times (with only 1 loss and 15 ties), one can surmise that he's still very sharp. Mustang comments that it's a waste to keep him stationed out in the provinces. Grumman is adept at disguising himself as an old woman.

He once worked in Central, but was sent to the Eastern Headquarters after flatly refusing Raven's invitation to join up with his Homunculus pals. Mustang has asked that Grumman help him stage a coup d'etat when the timing is right.

In the anime, he takes over leadership of the state when Bradley dies.

H

Hakuro

A Major General in the military. Hakuro has a rigid, by-the-numbers character. Originally working in New Optain, he is posted to the Eastern Headquarters. He's unhappy that Mustang has been promoted so fast so young. However, in his private life he cares about his family and is a good father. While taking his family on a vacation, he's kidnapped by Bald and gets part of his ear shot off.

Halling

An innkeeper and friend of the miners in Youswell. Despises State Alchemists. He has studied some alchemy, and believes it should be used for the public good. His

inn is burned down by Yoki, but thanks to Ed he receives the deed to the mines. He is helped by Mei Chan when the mine caves in.

Henry Douglas

A colonel in the military. He is a commander in the military police. He was in charge of the investingation into Ross in connection with Hughes death. When Ross breaks out of prison, he authorizes the use of deadly force against her, then paradoxically reprimands Mustang for going too far in his actions. He apparently disapproves of the fact that Mustang, who hails from the countryside, has made it so far up the ranks. Mustang feeds Douglas false reports that lead him to believe the Elric brothers are androids.

I

Izumi Curtis

An alchemist. Instructs the Elric brothers. Currently 35 years old. Has been married for 18 years. She describes herself as a "part-time housewife."

She has distinctive tiny braids that she wears in a ponytail and the mark of Flamel tattooed over her left collarbone. Despite her poor health, Izumi looks young and beautiful. However she dresses in fairly casual (albeit often revealing) clothes and is usually seen wearing cheap sandals, like the kind many Japanese keep for use in their bathrooms.

As an alchemy instructor she's very tough on the Elric brothers, but to them she's like a foster mother. The feeling is reciprocated--since Izumi has no children of her own, the Elrics are like adopted sons. Originally, she had a policy of not accepting pupils, but was swayed by the Elric brothers' determination.

In addition to being a talented alchemist, she is also a good enough martial artist to defeat much larger opponents one after another. In the anime, she knows a lot about the Homunculi, having made an attempt at the taboo art of human transmutation.

Her husband Sig is a butcher, and the two are very open about their affection, no matter where they are. Sadly, this love is related to her attempt at performing a human transmutation on her stillborn son, during which she lost a number of internal organs. As a result she can no longer have children and suffers from a frail constitution and occasional bouts of coughing up blood.

In the anime, her alchemy instructor was Dante, and the Homunculus Wrath was

created during Izumi's attempt at ressurecting her son. She plays a more central role in the anime than in the manga.

J

Jean Havoc

A second lieutenant (currently retired due to war injuries). Roy Mustang's subordinate.

Although exemplary in his sense of duty and highly trusted by his subordinates, Havoc has a somewhat ineffective personality, which prevents him from being promoted. His trademark is a dangling cigarette. He is proficient in the art of war, and after Riza, is the subordinate who helps Roy the most during battle. His luck with women is awful. On transferring to Central, Armstrong introduces his sister to Havoc, but she rejects him on the grounds that her ideal man is her brother. Havoc does make a girlfriend in Central, but it turns out to be Lust who is spying on Roy by getting close to him. In the battle with Lust, Havoc suffers a spinal injury. Although not fatal, he is left a paraplegic and retires from the military.

Joliot Comanche

A State Alchemist also known as the Silver Alchemist. A diminutive, elderly man with a silk hat and beard. He has a pegleg, having lost his left leg in Ishbal. He has transmutation circles inscribed on both hands with which he transmutes various edged weapons, such as swords and chakra. He is killed by Scar, who manages to knock off his pegleg and kill him.

Juliet Douglas

Only appears in the anime. Executive assistant to the Fuhrer. She is actually Sloth in disguise. She looks like the Elric brothers' mother Trisha.

Military records show that twice before someone with this name was enlisted, but died in both cases. She is said to have fired the shot that started the war with Ishbal.

K

Kain Fuery

A master sergeant in the military. One of Roy Mustang's subordinates. He has a boyish face and wears glasses. He's mild, kind and a bit of wimp. A communications specialist, he sends external signals to lure the Homunculi out. He takes in the

abdoned dog, Black Hayate.

He is now working in the Southern Headquarters on Bradley's orders. He is named after the Hawker Fury, a British aircraft of the 1930s. Unlike the rest of Mustang's subordinates, he is an enlisted soldier.

Karin

Majahal's lover. Only appears in the anime. Twenty years prior to the story arc, she lost her memory in an accident. She eventually regains her memory and returns home, but Majahal doesn't recognize her. Even when the truth is revealed to him, Majahal rejects her. She lives under the alias Lebi on returning home.

Kayal

Halling's son. Kayal is saved from Yoki by Ed. When he finds Mei Chan collapsed, he helps her by giving her a boxed lunch.

King Bradley

The military's Commander-in-Chief. He is the highest authority in Amestris.

His numerous exploits on the battlefield allow him to gain his title of Fuhrer at the young age of 44. Currently 60 years old. He has a patch over his left eye. He created the State Alchemist system after becoming Fuhrer. This served to concen-trate political power with the central government, and through military intervention in other countries and suppression of domestic uprisings, the military became deeply involved in politics. He is actually a Homunculus (Wrath in the manga, Pride in the anime), which may explain why he became Fuhrer at such a young age.

He has something of a split personality. Although he's a cold realist at heart, he can also be a good-natured old man. For example, he secretly visits Ed when he's laid up. He also puts on a Hawaiian shirt and takes Ed to Dublith with only Armstrong as a bodyguard. However, his ruthlessness emerges when he's revealed to be a Homunculus during the battle with Greed.

He was formerly a normal human. From childhood he was raised as an elite as part of the Homunculi's schemes. He was then turned into a Homunculus by being injected with a Philosopher's Stone. As a result, he ages unlike the other Homunculi (as a result, his powers decline somewhat with old age). His preferred weapon is the sword.

Knox

A coroner. He was a military doctor up until the Ishbal genocide. His experience in Ishbal left him prone to guilt and neu-

roses which trigger nightmares and insomnia (probably symptoms of post traumatic stress). As a result he leaves his wife and kids, retires from the military, and takes up practice as a coroner (currently it's unclear whether he still has ties with the military).

He has been a friend of Mustang since the war, and helps Ross escape by identifying her "corpse," although he realizes it's bogus. He has shown up since then to treat Ran Fan and Mei Chan.

L

Leo

A boy from Ishbal. Rick's older brother. Only appears in the anime. His mother is an Ishbalan. Very protective of his little brother.

Ling Yao

The Xing Emperor's twelfth son. He is from the Yao clan, which consists of 500,000 people. When the emperor falls ill, Ling and Fu are ordered to illegally enter Amestris to find a means of obtaining immortality in an attempt to boost the prestige of the Yao clan. He always keeps a smile on his face. This makes him seem friendly and light-hearted, but he's cool, collected, and not too fussy about how he achieves his goals. He truly believes that becoming the emperor will be good for his clan and his country. He is an excellent martial artist and possesses sword skills good enough to make even King Bradley howl in frustration.

Picked up when he collapsed in Rush Valley by Al. Ling figures out that the two know about the Philosopher's Stone, and goes along with them (not necessarily with their consent) to Central. There they encounter the Homunculi, whose regenerative power leads Ling to believe that they may provide a hint about immortality. He eventually finds his way to Father, the Homunculi creator. Father infuses him with a Philosopher's Stone, creating a new Greed. However, Ling's soul still lives on in his body along with Greed's soul. It seems Ling is plotting to take control back from Greed.

Ling has been trained in the aesthetic practices of his people, and as a result can sense the energy that flows within living things. As a result, he can detect beings in which this energy is absent, such as Al, Number 66, the Homunculi, etc. This ability servers him well when fighting the Homunculi.

Livia

Lujon's fiancée. Only appears in the anime. Two years before the story arc, she was saved from the Fossil Disease by Lujon. Heartbroken at seeing Lujon's corpse, she touches it. Because Lujon's body is infested with the Fossil Disease virus, she too becomes infected and dies in a few seconds.

Loa

One of Greed's subordinates. He's a bull/human chimera. Originally a soldier during the Ishbal war. He can transform into a Minotaur-like monster. His weapon is a large hammer. He specializes in charging attacks, but isn't that fast (Dorchet calls him the "beef bullet"). During the attack on Devil's Nest he fights Armstrong, with whom he's pretty evenly matched, but is finally killed by Bradley.

In the anime, it's revealed that he was in the Special Forces with Dorchet and Martel. He can be seen fighting in Ishbal during war flashback sequences.

Lujon

Only appears in the anime. A doctor who researches alchemy to try to save his hometown from the Fossil Disease (a rare disease that makes its victims bodies harden like withered trees). He receives an incomplete Philosopher's Stone from Lust that he uses to heal people. He falls in love with Lust, but she has thrown off her human past, and the episode ends tragically, with Lust killing him. After this, his corpse becomes infected by the Fossil Disease virus.

Lust

One of the Homunculi. Her appearance is that of a beautiful woman, with an Ouroboros insignia on her chest. She can extend her fingernails, which become sharp blades, tha she can fully control. The power of this weapon has earned her the name "Ultimate Lance."

Lyra

An alchemist. Only appears in the anime. She is determined to become a State Alchemist for her country and the military, but after losing to Ed reconsiders her stance, and becomes Dante's pupil. It seems she passes her time with Dante pleasantly, even learning at last how to smile. However, Lyra is betrayed; Dante simply wants to use her as her next vessel.

M

Mäes Hughes

A major in the military (promoted to brigadier general posthumously).

A close friend of Roy. He dotes on his family, and brags about them, particularly his daughter, to anyone, anywhere, even using military lines during work. Although this can be obnoxious, it helps him become closer to his subordinates. He is a quick thinker and an expert at using knives. In the anime, he is fond of the Elric brothers and looks out for them. He is killed by the Homunculi for discovering their plans. In the end, he is helpless against Envy, who assumes the form of his wife and daughter Elysia.

In the manga, he never meets the Elric brothers. He first meets the Elrics working for Hakuro and chats with them. In the anime, they become friends through the train hijacking incident.

Majahal

An alchemist. Only appears in the anime. Lives in a town that is apparently unnamed in the English translation, but called Linta in the Japanese version. Friend of Hohenheim. Learns alchemy to resurrect his lover Karin. Majahal tries to

kill Ed, but ends up dying on the point of his own sword.

Maria Ross

A second lieutenant in the military. Armstrong's subordinate. She has a mole under her left eye. She is one of the soldiers assigned to act as the Elric brothers' bodyguard. She regards Ed and Al as very important.

In the manga, Envy takes on Maria's form to attack Hughes, causing Maria to be thrown in jail. Mustang helps her fake her own death. Currently she lives in exile in Xing. She is prepared to make sacrifices, as shown by the fact that she hasn't even told her parents that she's alive.

In the anime, she restrains Ed, who has gone berserk in reaction to the Red Water, by hugging him. She also acts as a sort of mother figure to Ed, sometimes scolding him like a parent would.

Martel

One of Greed's subordinates. She's a snake/human chimera. Originally a member of the military. Her snake half allows her to disconnect her joints at will. Using this, she is able to slip inside Al's armor. Her weapon is a knife. Killed by Bradley during the attack on Devil's Nest.

In the anime, she survives the Devil's

Nest raid and joins the Elric brothers. She wants revenge on Kimblee for betraying Greed, and on King Bradley, but as in the manga she is impaled and killed by Bradley, even though she is inside Al's armor.

Mason

Employee at the butcher's shop. A strapping man who wears a towel wrapped around his head. Creates a sunny mood wherever he goes. As part of the Elric brothers' training, he plays the role of masked man and attacks Ed and Al. He is the exact opposite of Sig--talkative and cheerful.

Mei Chan

The Xing Emperor's seventeenth daughter. A Rentan Jutsu master. She is from the Chan clan, a family that has little sway with the Imperial court. She is Ling's half-sister. Like Ling, she has crossed the desert to Amestris to find a means of obtaining immortality to help her clan. Accompanying her is Xiao-Mei, her diminutive panda. As a Rentan Jutsu expert, she uses two formula circles (one near her, one near her target) to perform ranged techniques. Although small, Mei is adept at martial arts and easily defends herself against chimera. She harbors a fierce animosity toward the Yao clan, but her stance softens a bit after Knox admonishes her.

She uses her Rentan Jutsu to save the miners at Youswell after a cave-in. She decides to seek out Ed having heard rumors about him and tracks him to Central. However, on the way there she collapses and is picked up by Yoki and Scar.

Mister Han

A man who "coordinates" immigration and emigration. He helps Ling illegally enter Amestris. At Fu's request, he helps Ross find asylum in Xing.

Mrs. Bradley

King Bradley's wife and Selim's mother. She obviously worries about her husband, who is around 60, suggesting that he turn the reins of power over to someone else. While she unquestioningly supports her husband in his professional life, she apparently regards him as a complete idiot when it comes to women. Neither she nor her son know King Bradley's true form.

Mugwar

A very big landowner from Xenotime. Only appears in the anime. Has the

Tringum brothers research Red Water for him, even though he knows this is dangerous.

N

Nash Tringum

Russell and Fletcher's father. Only appears in the anime. Researches "Red Water" in order to create experimental Philosopher's Stones. Destroys his research when he discovers that Red Water is toxic to humans. He is forced to continue his research against his will by Mugwar.

Nina Tucker

Shou Tucker's daughter. She's a very energetic girl and loves her father very much. Shou Tucker, under pressure of the evaluation, turns her and Alexander into a chimera. He and the chimera are later killed by Scar.

In the anime, she lived in Central three years before the story arc with her father, who was taking the State Alchemist exam. Hearing that Basque Grand is going to institutionalize her in a laboratory, she panics and escapes with some help from Ed. She's killed by scar while hiding on a back street. Later, Shou Tucker manages

to perfectly reconstruct her body, but it has no soul.

O

Olivier Mila Armstrong

A major general in the military. Armstrong's older sister. Garrisoned in the Northern Headquarters, she protects the boarder with Drachma, an area also known as Brigg's Cliff. Like her younger sister, she is a stunning beauty who bears no resemblance whatsoever to her brother.

P

Paninya

A resident of Rush Valley. There she is a notorious pickpocket. As a child, she lost her legs in an accident, so Dominic fitted her with automail legs with hidden weapons (a cannon and a knife). She originally plans to pay Dominic back with earnings from her thievery, but sees the error of her ways after Winry lectures her. She has since switched to repairing roofs to pay back her debt. She has a phobia of blood, due to her past trauma. Friends with Al. On fighting Fu in Rush Valley, she

demonstrates combos even more advanced than those performed by Ed.

In the anime, she has also lost her arm and is Dominic's adopted child.

Phillip Gargantos Armstrong

Armstrong's father. His appearance is very similar to his son. He was once a general, but doesn't appear to know anything about the truth behind the Fuhrer of Father. He constantly brags about the Armstrong name. He's short, but very stocky.

Pinako Rockbell

A practitioner of external medicine and an automail technician. Winry's grandmother. Runs an automail shop in Risembool with Winry. Often seen smoking a kiseru pipe. Although she and Ed often get into arguments, she loves Ed and Al dearly. When their mother (Trisha Elric) dies, Pinako takes them in and looks after them like her own family.

Some 40 years prior to the story arc, she was known as the "Leopardess of Risembool" and widely feared for her violent temper. Even the strapping Dominic was terrified of her. She was apparently quite a beauty in those days, but how she got so short is a mystery. She was Hohenheim's drinking buddy for a number of decades, during which she realized that his appearance never changed.

Pride

One of the Homunculi. His appearance is completely different in the manga and anime.

He was the first Homunculus created. He at first appears only as a voice.

Although he has not yet been shown, he is distinguished in the manga by the rather polite language he uses (at least in the Japanese version). His ability to silence Envy seems to indicate he is in a leadership position among the Homunculi. In the anime, Pride is actually King Bradley. It is unclear who his human base is. His appearance and abilities are identical to those of the King Bradley character in the manga.

R

Ran Fan

A young woman who belongs to a family that has served Ling's household for generations. She is a beautiful girl, but somewhat introverted and prone to blushing. She often wears a black mask. Like Ling and Fu, she is a highly skilled martial

artist and specializes in kunai (throwing knife) techniques. She adores Ling, and will not suffer any insult to him. As a result, the way she treats Ling is completely different from the way she treats everyone else (particularly Ed and Mei Chan). In the capture of Gluttony, the trap she sets for Wrath is similar to the one Ed previously used on her. When her left arm becomes injured, she cuts it off and uses it as a decoy to escape. She leaves Central temporarily to look for an automail replacement for her arm.

Raven

A lieutenant general in the military. A member of the upper echelon of the military. He's late middle-aged, bearded and tanned. He seems easygoing and generous, but like all members of the military elite he has sold out to the Homunculi. Consequently, he knows that King Bradley is a Homunculus.

Rick

A boy from Ishbal. In the anime, he's Leo's younger brother. Saves Scar from Lust and Gluttony. His mother is an Ishbalan.

Riddle LeCoulte

An automail mechanic. Dominic's son. Unlike his father, Riddle has a flexible world view. Introduces Winry to Garfiel.

Riza Hawkeye

Roy Mustang's subordinate. In the manga she is currently working directly under the Fuhrer as his aid.

She's an attractive woman with blond hair and dark brown eyes. She is always calm, collected, and virtually never shows her feelings. At heart she is a kind woman, as demonstrated by the way she adopts Black Hayate, an abandoned dog. She is an excellent shot, and this talent was put to use in battle while she was still a cadet. She is said to truly have "the eyes of a hawk." She always carries multiple firearms, usually an FN Browning M1910 and Enfield No. 2.

She has a tattoo on her back which contains an encoded alchemic secret discovered by her father. After the Ishbal war, she decides this secret should be destroyed, and has Roy partially burn it. As mentioned above, she is currently working directly under Bradley, probably so she can be used as leverage against Roy.

Rose Thomas

A woman from Lior. Follower of the Leto religion. She became deeply depressed

when her lover died, and joined the Leto faith because she hopes it will resurrect him. However, she loses hope when the Elric brothers expose Cornello, her spiritual leader, as a fraud.

In the anime, she's an Ishbalan (although her eye color is not typical of the Ishbalans, suggesting she might be of mixed heritage). During the Lior insurrection, she's arrested by the military and assaulted. When she returns, she has a child by an unknown father and no longer speaks. Interestingly, Hiromu Arakawa, the author of the manga, has expressed discomfort with this aspect of Rose's character in the anime. Later Scar, who plans to make a Philosopher's Stone using a transmutation circle he has drawn around the town of Lior, dubs her the Holy Mother and elevates her as an example to the people of Lior. After Lior is wiped out, she is brainwashed by Lust.

Roy Mustang

Starts as a captain during the extermination at Ishbal, and rises to major (during the Ishbal extermination), lieutenant colonel (around the time Ed passes the State Alchemist test), colonel, and brigadier general (from the 46th episode of the anime). A State Alchemist also known as the Flame Alchemist.

At first blush he seems a rakish womanizer, but he's actually strong-willed and crafty. He is stern, but also kind. Having experienced the Ishbal war, he wants to create a better world for the next generation. Therefore he aspires to become Fuhrer in order to change his country's political system. Although he normally gives top priority to his mission, when someone close to him is in trouble he acts with no thought of danger to himself.

As his nick-name implies, he has a talent for fire techniques. He uses alchemy to generate the three elements necessary for fire--a combustible material, oxygen and a source of ignition. He uses the target as the combustible material, and enriches the oxygen content of the surrounding air using alchemy. The spark for igniting it is created by his gloves, which are made of a material called pyrotex that produces sparks from friction. He learns that King Bradley is really a Homunculus, and that even if he rises through the ranks of the military, the military's upper echelon will always be under the sway of the Homunculi. In the manga, Mustang is currently isolated. All his loyal subordinates have been scattered throughout the various bases by Bradley, and Mustang's confidant, Riza, has been assigned to work directly under the Fuhrer.

In the anime, unlike the manga, he is forced by Brigadier General Grand to kill Winry's parents. This traumatizes him deeply. Due to this trauma, he is never able to use a gun again, except as a means of intimidation. He wants to use human transmutation to resurrect everyone killed during the Ishbal conflict, but his friend Hughes talks him out of it. At the end of the anime, he manages to defeat Bradley. Ironically, Archer shoots Mustang in the eye, and he must wear an eye patch like the one Bradley wore.

Russell Tringum

An alchemist. Fletcher's brother. Only appears in the anime. Poses as Ed. Has an arrogant personality. Later tells Ed about the underground city that his father, Nash, had written about in his diary. Taller than Ed, but younger.

S

Sara Rockbell

Winry's mother. A practitioner of external medicine and an automail technician. Marries Yuri, Pinako's son, in 1898. Together with her husband, she provides medical care in Ishbal. However, they are senselessly murdered (in the manga, it is Scar that kills them while in the anime it is Mustang).

Satella LeCoulte

Riddle's wife. She goes into labor during a terrible downpour, but thanks to Winry delivers the child safely.

Scar

A man from Ishbal. An alchemist. Has a cross-shaped scar on his forehead. He has the characteristic brown skin and red eyes (which he usually hides with sunglasses) of the Ishbalans. Originally a monk, he begins killing State Alchemists to avenge the Ishbal extermination, during which his brother and countrymen died. His real name is unknown--Scar is the name the military uses when referring to him.

The Ishbalan doctrine abhors alchemy, a fact that created conflict between Scar and his older brother who was reasearching it. During the Ishbal genocide, Kimblee attacks Scar, but his brother saves him by acting as a human shield. Scar is not killed, but loses his arm. His brother, severely wounded, saves Scar by transplanting his own right arm.

Scar was powerful to begin with--monks of Ishbal are each said to be worth about 10 Amestris soldiers, and have highly

developed martial arts. Adding to this, the arm his brother gave him contained a transmutation circle capable of performing the Decomposing step of alchemy (in the anime, it could perform Reconstruction too). Using this, Scar can disintegrate people and objects.

In the anime, Scar creates a Philosopher's Stone for Al by transmuting himself and 7000 Amestris soldiers. In the anime he's a bit younger and more handsome than in the manga. His personality is also slightly different.

Selim Bradley

King Bradley's son. He very much wants to meet Ed, who's about the same age as him. Upon finally meeting the Elric brothers, he's overjoyed. Is dedicated to his studies.

In the anime, he unwittingly brings out the skull that is his father's weakness. Furious, King Bradley strangles him.

Shan

An old Ishbalan woman. She stops the youths who attack Ed. During the Ishbal genocide, the Rockbells gave her medical care. She is one of the few people who knows of the Rockbell's death. She continually regrets that she couldn't prevent their deaths.

Sheska

Rank unknown. Subordinate of Hughes and Focker (manga only). She works at the court-martial hall. She wears a uniform, but it's unclear where she's officially posted. Nicknamed "the bookworm" (although she herself dislikes this name). She's timid and has little self-confidence, considering her own skills useless until she meets Ed. She develops some self-confidence after a pep-talk from Al.

Her love for books goes beyond the pale of a mere hobby. She memorizes everything she reads, and learns everything in Marcoh's data on Philosopher's Stones before it's destroyed.

In the manga, she starts out working at the nation's central library, but is fired due to her extreme love of books (she's always reading on the job). When Sheska meets the Elric brothers, she's looking for a job to help out her ill mother. She helps the Elrics and with the money they give her (quite a lot, apparently) is able to get medical care for her mom. She meets Hughes through the Elrics, and he puts her special talents to use in the military courts. When Mustang is posted to Central, she helps him out by leaving the archives open.

In the anime, she finds Hughes' death suspicious and investigates it herself. She

is fairly important to the story, and at one point she even infiltrates the core of the military with Winry.

Shou Tucker

A State Alchemist also known as the Sewing Life Alchemist. An alchemist who lived in East City with his daughter and their dog. He claims his wife has run away, but in fact he used her to create a "talking chimera" to obtain his State Alchemist license. The success of this experiment earned him a reputation as a chimera expert. His impatience to produce more research results leads him to create a chimera using his daughter, Nina. The Elric brothers figure out what he's been up to, and have him taken into custody. After being in custody, Shou is ordered to stay at home, but is attacked by Scar and killed along with Nina and Alexander.

In the anime, his role is close to Marcoh. As a result, it's feared that he will reveal military secrets, so he is quickly sentenced to death. However, in fact his knowledge is put to use making chimeras for the military (Homunculi). He later withdraws from the military to attempt to resurrect his daughter Nina. Learning that Al has been turned into a Philosopher's Stone, Shou tries to use him for a human transmutation. He succeeds only in creat-

ing an empty doll in Nina's image, and becomes mentally unstable having lost all hope. In the anime Edward has a deeper relationship with him than in the manga. Shou even hosts Ed while he studies for the State Alchemist exam.

Sig Curtis

Izumi's husband. Owns a butcher shop in Dublith which he runs with Izumi. He feels regret for not being able to do anything for Izumi when she lost her baby. He and Armstrong bonded by comparing muscles. While he looks old, he's actually fairly young, being just one year older than Izumi (when they met, he was 19; now he's 36). He is self-conscious about his scary appearance.

Slicer Brothers (Number 48)

An assassin who guards Laboratory 5 Number 48 is a suit of armor in which the souls of two brothers are sealed. The elder brother is sealed in the head, while the younger is sealed into the torso. They use a sword similar to a Japanese katana. Their exquisite swordsmanship nearly overwhelms Ed. in the manga, they are defeated by Ed, but killed by Lust and Envy to prevent them from divulging any information.

In the anime, the younger brother inten-

tionally scrapes off his Blood Seal, while the older brother is killed by Lust to intimidate Ed.

Sloth

One of the Homunculi. Like Wrath, Sloth's appearance is completely different in the manga and anime.

She was the fifth Homunculus to be created. Her Ouroboros insignia is on her left shoulder. In the manga as of yet he's only appeared in two panels so it's difficult to tell what he looks like.

He appears to be huge and muscular. He has been digging some sort of hole or tunnel for 100 years, but as his name suggests he frequently slacks off, and as a result hasn't finished whatever his task is.

In the anime, Sloth is a very different character. Her Ouroboros insignia is on her left breast. She is based on Trisha, the Elrics' mother. Her alias is Colonel Juliet Douglas, private secretary to King Bradley.

Storche

A manga-only character, he is Bradley's secretary. He and Yakovlev inform Hawkeye and the others of their transfers. He shows up during King Bradley's visit to the front and when Ed takes the State Alchemist exam.

T

Tim Marcoh

Formerly a State Alchemist also known as the Crystal Alchemist. He was involved in the creation of Philosopher's Stones at a military alchemic research center. However, he's appalled that the material for the stones is living humans and that the finished prototypes are used by death squads in Ishbal. He steals his data and prototypes and flees. He changes his name to Mauro and goes into hiding, working as a country doctor. After meeting the Elric brothers, he gives them a hint regarding the secret of the Philosopher's Stones. At the same time, he's found by Lust, who holds the town hostage. The Elrics manage to confine the Homunculus. After this, he meets Scar and tells him about the Ishbal war. He and Scar then run from the Homunculi. Scar disfigures part of Marcoh's face to conceal his identity.

In the anime, Marcoh is captured by the military and eventually killed .

Trisha Elric

The Elric brothers' mother. She raised the brothers herself. Trisha has a gentle personality. Pining for her absent lover

Hohenheim (in the manga, they never officially marry), she becomes ill and dies young. It seems she forgave (or perhaps completely understood) Hohenheim's sudden departure, and continued to love him without any resentment. In the manga, in her final words she apologizes to Hohenheim for not keeping up her end of an as of yet unknown promise.

In the anime, she becomes the Homunculus Sloth.

U

Ulchi

One of Greed's subordinates. He's a crocodile/human chimera. Originally a member of the military. Little is revealed about his personality, other than he loves women. Tries to rush Izumi, but gets beaten up by Sig. Eventually killed during the raid on Devil's Nest.

V

Van Hohenheim

The Elric brothers' real father. An alchemist.

He's distinguished by his blond hair, glasses and goatee. He met Trisha in Risembool where they had two sons together, but suddenly disappears looking for something he had been long searching for (in the anime, it's a way to prevent his body from decaying). Ed feels strong resentment towards his father for leaving Trisha, and not even coming to her funeral (Al has almost no memory of his father and doesn't hold any ill-will toward him.) He never formally married Trisha, and therefore there are no official documents connecting the two (the records seem to have bee erased). Ten years after leaving Hohenheim at last returns home to learn that Trisha has died some six years before, and Ed has burned their house down. He stays a few days with his old friend Pinako and meets the now grown-up Ed, but the two don't get along.

He's a mysterious man, who never seems to age even over tens of years and doesn't die even when riddled with bullets. He refers to himself as a "monster." In the manga, the character called Father, who lives beneath the military base, seems to know him well, and the two look somewhat similar, so it seems likely that Hohenheim will play an important role in the story hereafter.

His character in the anime is quite different from the manga. He's called "Hohenheim of Light" and has lived about

400 years by moving his soul between various host bodies, as has Dante. However, his body is beginning to decay, albeit at a slower rate than Dante's (it seems that when changing bodies, he ages slightly). Trying to reason with Dante (Lyra), he is pushed through the Gate into the "real" world.

Vato Falman

A warrant officer in the military. One of Roy Mustang's subordinates. He's a skinny man with hallow cheeks. His primary skill is his database-like memory. Originally attended the Northern Military Academy. He eventually moves east and is placed under Mustang's command. He is put in charge of interrogating Number 66 (Barry the Chopper), and is ordered to guard him. In the manga, he has been reassigned to the Northern Headquarters by Bradley.

W

Wrath

One of the Homunculi. His appearance is completely different in the manga and anime.

In the manga he was the seventh Homunculus created. He is actually King Bradley. His Ouroboros insignia is on his left eye.

In the anime, Sloth is a very different character. His Ouroboros insignia is on the sole of his right foot. He is based on Izumi's child. After being born from a human transmutation, he was sent to the other side of the Gate where he grew up.

Winry Rockbell

A young girl with blue eyes and blond hair. Originally from Risembool, she is a childhood friend of Ed and Al. Born to a family of medical practitioners, as a child she whiled away her free time reading medical texts. Both her parents died when she was eight during the Ishbal conflict. She was raised by her grandmother Pinako. Due to Pinako's influence, she becomes an automail mechanic. Winry has an innate talent for mechanics, and she builds and installs all of Ed's automail herself. Ed seems to want no one other than Winry to work on his automail--he returns to Risembool for repairs and installation, and sometimes calls Winry into the field when he needs maintenance. Having been brought up in a family of doctors, she also has a very good understanding of medicine, and in one episode volunteers to act as a midwife.

X

Xiao-Mei

Mei's companion (a female panda). In the manga, it's explained that Xiao-Mei is a normal panda who fell ill as a cub and stopped growing. Her behavior is odd for a panda--she seems to understand human language and is sometimes seen swilling down flagons of beer. Xiao-Mei is fiercely loyal to her mistress, and will bite anyone who threatens her.

Xing Emperor

The ruler of Xing, a country with over 50 ethnic groups. The father of 24 princes and 19 princesses. In the manga series, he is currently ill.

Y

Yakovlev

Rank unknown. Works at the Personnel Affairs Department. He appears along with Storch in the scene where they inform Hawkeye of her transfer

Yoki

Originally a lieutenant in the military. A very corrupt man who isn't picky about how he gets what he wants. He administered the mines at Youswell, and levied heavy taxes on the people which he then gave to the higher public officials as bribes. He is tricked by Ed into signing over the management rights of the mines. When word of his oppression of the town reaches the Eastern Command Center, Yoki is dismissed.

He's taken in by an Ishbalan refugee camp, but gets tossed out for trying to turn in Scar, who's also sheltering there, for the reward money. In the manga, he is currently employed by Scar as his servant. Some of his recent lines seem to indicate concern for Scar, perhaps showing that Yoki is starting to mend his ways.

In the anime, he was Lyra's original master. Also, in the anime Yoki lives in the refugee camp after being tricked by Ed, but is eventually killed by the Homunculi.

Yuri Rockbell

Winry's father. Surgeon. Marries Sara in 1898. As dedicated doctors, he and his wife give medical treatment to people injured during the Ishbal conflict, whether they are friend or foe. This endears them to the Ishbalans. However, they are senselessly murdered (in the manga, it is Scar that kills them while in the anime it is Mustang). He is 35 when he dies.

Z

Zolf J. Kimblee

A major in the military (promoted to lieutenant colonel). A State Alchemist also known as the Crimson Alchemist.

He has transmutation circles tattooed on his palms, allowing him to use his alchemy by clapping his hands. He can use this to turn anything he touches into an explosive substance. He has extensive knowledge of explosives, earning him the nickname "Mad Bomber Kimblee" (translated from the Japanese). Although deporting himself like a gentleman, he is a cold-blooded killer with no respect for human life. During the Ishbal war, he uses his own troops as human shields against incoming shells. He is an extremely evil character, on a par with Envy. Despite being a psychopath, it seems he passed the State Alchemist exam by sneaking through the psychiatric evaluation.

Although he fought in the Ishbal war, he was sentenced to death for indiscriminately killing friend and foe alike. Kimblee was the one who gave Scar his x-shaped scar. After the Ishbal war, he refuses to give up his Philosopher's Stone, and blows up the superior officer who was sent to collect it. His disposition and actions make him a natural ally of the Homunculi. He's imprisoned for killing his superior, but is released to assist in the capture of Marcoh, destroy a town to make an example of it, and kill Scar.

In the anime, he works with Greed for awhile, but betrays him in order to regain his commission in the military. After this, he is put under Archer's command. He fights Scar in Lior and although he manages to transmute Scar's arm into a bomb, Scar removes it himself. Kimblee is stabbed and dies. However, as he's dying he transmutes Al's body into a bomb.

GLOSSARY

A

Alchemist

Someone who uses alchemy. There is a saying among alchemists that "alchemists work for the people," but in fact the best alchemists often end up taking the government sponsored license and becoming State Alchemists. State Alchemists are sometimes referred to as "dogs of the military" by the public since they serve the military, not the people. Some of them are very close to what we would call scientists.

Alchemy

The art of decomposing and reconstructing objects through understanding laws and currents.

Aono Dan (the Blue Team)

A group of extremists. They hijack the train Hakuro is on. At the time, they were lead by Bald. Currently, their leader is in the custody of the military, and though he demanded his team rescue him, they were thwarted by Ed. In the end, Bald was turned to ash by Roy's alchemy.

Atelier Garfiel

An automail shop run by Garfiel, Winry's instructor in Rush Valley. Winry helps Garfiel with the shop, and in return he teaches her about automail.

Automail

A kind of mechanical prosthetic limb that is connected directly to the user's nervous system. Can be moved as freely as the user's natural limbs, but the process of attaching them is very painful and learning to use them requires some rehab time.

B

Briggs Mountain

Mountain near the border of Amestris and Drachma. Its natural environment has been left pretty much unspoiled. Bears are sometimes sighted there. In her younger days, Izumi Curtis once lived there as part of her alchemist training.

C

Central City

Amestris' most important city. Home to many important national institutions. All the major military institutions are in this city.

Central Headquarters

Located in Central City, it houses the national government. It is directly administered by the Fuhrer and also contains the State Alchemist headquarters.

Chimera

A living being created through alchemy by fusing multiple living things.

Creta

Country that lies to the west of Amestris. There are constant border skirmishes between it and Amestris.

Crimson Alchemist

Title given to the State Alchemist known as Kimblee. Uses explosive techniques.

D

Devil's Nest

A bar in Dublith. The base of operations for the Homunculus named Greed.

Dublith

A town in the south of Amestris. Izumi Curtis, the Elric brothers' instructor, lives here and operates a butcher's shop with her husband Sig.

E

East City

A city in the east of Amestris. Location of the Eastern Headquarters where Roy Mustang works.

F

Fifth Laboratory

Although a military facility, research into the secrets of the Philosopher's Stone is also being secretly carried out here. Guarded by Number 48 and Number 66. Basque Grand is in charge of the place.

Flame Alchemist
Title given to the State Alchemist Roy Mustang.

Flamel Insignia
Insignia worn by the Elric brothers. Izumi Curtis has this insignia on her chest. Seems to indicate the branch of alchemy to which Izumi and the Elric brothers belong.

H

Human Transmutation
Refers to the act of transmuting a human through alchemy. It is a taboo act due to the extreme danger involved (it requires a very high trade-off under the Law of Equivalent Exchange). It can be performed safely only with a Philosopher's Stone.

I

Ishbal
A place located northeast of East City. Home to the Ishbalan people. Devastated during the war with Amestris.

Ishbalan War
A war that started out as a series of skir-

mishes between Ishbal and Amestris, but escalated when an Amestris solider accidentally killed an Ishbalan child. The military deployed State Alchemists, who managed to pacify the area, but reduced it to ruins in the process. The war was actually started intentionally by the military as part of their Philosopher's Stone research, which required a large number of human lives.

Ishbalan people
Refers to the citizens of Ishbal. They have brown skin and red eyes. They believe in a single god called Ishbala. The people are left in ruin by a war with Amestris, called the Ishbalan War. Now only a few Ishbalans survive, and are living in poverty. Scar is one such citizen of Ishbal.

K

Kauroy Lake
A lake in Dublith, where the Elric brothers study under Izumi Curtis. A famous tourist attraction. In the middle of the lake is a deserted island called Yock Island. Here the Elric brothers took a survival test in order to be accepted as Izumi's pupils.

L

Law of Equivalent Exchange

A crucial law related to the performing of alchemy. Put simply, when an alchemist turns one object into another, she follows the formula "object + alchemy = created object." The more elaborate the created object, the higher the level of alchemy required. If the alchemist attempts a transmutation beyond her skill, the "level difference" must be made up by way of a trade-off. In some cases this is a body part, or even the alchemist's life.

Leto

The "god" Cornello invokes to trick the people of Lior. Cornello performs "miracles" with alchemy in front of the citizens to foster faith in this god. Since the founder of this religion is himself a fraud, it's unknown what kind of god Leto is and what his teachings might be. It is very likely that this god is a fabrication of Cornello's.

Leto Religion

A new religion devoted to the sun-god Leto. The religion's founder Father Cornello uses a Philosopher's Stone to perform "miracles" and gather followers in Lior.

Lior

An independent country located to the east of Amestris. Its citizens look a lot like the Ishbalans. It is here that Father Cornello uses a Philosopher's Stone to perform "miracles" and gather followers. The town even goes so far as to build a large church devoted to Leto. Eventually Cornello's fraud is discovered and the town rises up against him.

Living Transmutation

Technique that allows the recreation of a lost limb, etc. using alchemy. Unlike human transmutation, it is not forbidden and is used by many researchers.

N

National Library

One of the military institutions in Central City. The largest repository of documents in the country. Has several branch libraries. The First Branch contains various books on alchemy until a suspicious fire destroys them.

New Optain

A town in the east of Amestris. Hakuro is

responsible for administering it.

Number 48

Like Alphonse, a suit of armor animated by a pair of souls bound to it by a blood seal. The souls belong to the "Slicer Brothers," a pair of assassins.

Number 66

Like Alphonse, a suit of armor animated by a pair of souls bound to it by a blood seal. The soul is that of Barry the Chopper, a former serial killer.

O

Ouroboros

A design found somewhere on each of the Homunculi bodies. It depicts a dragon biting its own tail to form a circle. Visual representation of the expression "one is all, all is one."

P

Philosopher's Stone

A very rare item that allows one to perform alchemy that transcends the Law of Equivalent Exchange. Creating one requires many human souls.

Pyrotex

An artificial fabric that produces sparks with just a tiny amount of friction. Roy Mustang wears gloves made of this material so he can produce sparks for his fire alchemy anytime he wants.

R

Rentan Jutsu

An art similar to alchemy, developed in Xing. It's most powerful techniques are mainly medical.

Risembool

The country town where Edward and Alphonse Elric and Winry Rockbell were born. Because Edward burned down his own house, whenever the brothers return they stay at the Rockbell's house.

Rush Valley

A town in the south of Amestris. A number of excellent automail mechanics live here, and so the town's main industry is automail production.

S

Sewing Life Alchemist

Title given to Shou Tucker, a State Alchemist who specializes in creating chimeras.

State Alchemist

An alchemist who has special privileges and is attached to the military (directly administered by the central government). As a symbol of their status, State Alchemists are given a silver pocket watch bearing the coat of arms of their country. Each State Alchemist also receives a title from the Fuhrer. State Alchemists are reevaluated once a year, and those judged unfit have their status revoked.

Strong Arm Alchemist

The title given to State Alchemist Alex Louis Armstrong.

T

Transmutation

Technique used to reconstruct a new object through alchemy.

Transmutation Circle

A magic circle used by the alchemist to perform a transmutation. Power is focused into the center of the circle. A chemical formula (or something similar) is written around the edge of the circle. Any object placed in the center of the circle is broken down at the atomic level and reconstructed as a different object.

X

Xerxes Ruins

The ruins that lie in the desert between Amestris and Xing. A legend says that it was once a prosperous city, but that it was destroyed in a single night. An insignia can be seen in the ruins that looks very similar to the transmutation circle seen at the military's Fifth Laboratory (where Philosopher's Stones are being researched).

Xing

Country that lies to the far east of Amestris. Unlike the ostensibly democratic Amestris, Xing is ruled by a hereditary imperial bloodline. Xing has developed a system called Rentan Jutsu, which is similar to alchemy.

Y

Yock Island

A deserted island in the middle of Kauroy Lake, a popular tourist destination in Dublith. Here the Elric brothers took a one-month survival test in order to be accepted as Izumi's pupils. As a result, they learned the universal concept of "one is all, all is one."

Youswell

A mining town. The citizens are oppressed by Yoki, the official who runs the town.

KEYWORD INDEX

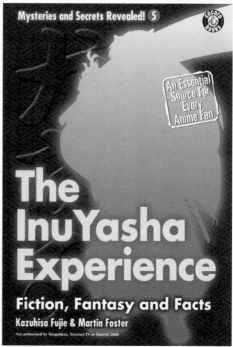

InuYasha Profile 001
Name: InuYasha

InuYasha is a demi-demon, born of a human mother and a demon father. Both parents died while he was still young. He is estimated to be 15 years of age, and leads a lonely existence, looked down upon by the demon full-bloods because he is only half demon and incapable of living as an ordinary human being.

As a result, he develops an independent, stand-alone view on life, saying "I will get whatever it is I want based entirely on my own merits." To achieve this, he reasons that he needs to become a full-blooded demon. He sets his mind on acquiring the Shikon jewel, which will see these wishes granted.

Things change when he meets Kagome. She is the first person he can really open up to, and he suddenly realizes that he wants to protect her, and so begins a new page in the emotional and mental development of our hero.

The tale of InuYasha, a mystical half-demon, and Kagome, a schoolgirl transported back in time from present-day Tokyo, is one of anime biggest hits. Set in Japan's ancient Era of Warring States, when demons and magic ruled, InuYasha is the story of a quest to find the shards of the broken Shikon jewel, and by doing so bring peace to the land and love to the protagonist and his modern-day princess.

192 pages packed with secrets, subplots, character traits, hidden meanings, behind-the-scenes gossip and little-known facts, **The InuYasha Experience** opens up a whole new world that anime fans never knew existed. Find out who did what when and why in one of the most popular anime ever released on either side of the Pacific!

InuYasha Goods 003

InuYasha Cell Phone Cover

Bandai, that fine purveyor of tie-in toys, has released a whole series of anime art for cell phones. Known as Chara Haru Art, the series would not be replete without InuYasha.

The concept is simple, and applying the design is easier than it looks. The kit consists of one colored transparent sheet and some clear tape. Simply cut the sheet and place one part over the outside of the phone, smooth it with your fingers and adhere with the tape. Any rough edges can be removed with a sharp knife.

Once that's complete, do the same for the inside of the phone. Cover the screen and push-buttons, stick and cut. The actual material is so clear and pliable that it doesn't affect visuals or working the number board. In fact, the artwork acts more like a wrapper, tightly encasing the phone so that it looks like it's been on there forever.

We chose the purple design, with InuYasha and Kagome on the back falling through the well. Emblazoned on the front are the InuYasha kanji characters. However, there are others designs in blossom pink and aquamarine that depict different characters and InuYasha striking other poses.

Bandai
$15.00

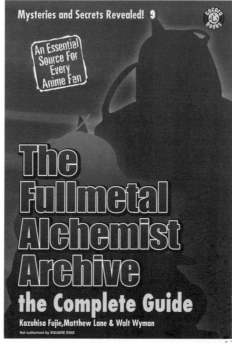